STRANGE SUDBURY STORIES
6 Speculative Tales by 3 Sudbury Authors

SEAN COSTELLO
MARK LESLIE
SCOTT OVERTON

Stark Publishing

STARK
PUBLISHING

This one's for the people of Sudbury.
Past, present, and future.

No matter where you now live, if you ever called
Sudbury your home, you have Sudbury in your blood
and Sudbury in your bones.

Table of Contents

SUDBURY, OH SUDBURY

Mark Leslie Lefebvre

There is a song, that still rings in the back of my mind like a persistent earworm that just won't let go.

If you're of a certain age, perhaps you remember it too.

Sudbury, oh Sudbury
You are always home to me
United, strong, and proud
Sudbury...

I think there's a reason why, even if I sometimes can't get the song from repeating in my mind, I fondly consider it with a good dose of nostalgia.

It's because Sudbury is an amazing place.

Unlike any I've ever lived or visited.

When I was young and growing up, I regarded the city of Sudbury with awe. And, as I've grown older, visited multiple continents, explored, and learned about the world beyond, I still regard Sudbury with a sense of awe and wonder.

When I was a teenager, and wanting, desperately, to leave for other places in the universe, to explore, discover, conquer all those vast areas beyond my home, I likely didn't feel the same.

But every time I returned back home I felt that natural click of belonging that often escaped me as a teen. And yes, home still is, and will always be, Sudbury. Well, Levack, which, at the time, was part of the town of Onaping Falls was technically my home. But that town is no more, and is now pretty much a "suburb" of the City of Greater Sudbury.

It's funny. When I was young, Sudbury was the big city to me.

The town I grew up in didn't even have a single traffic light. Oh, it did have one of those red blinking lights suspended in the odd six-way intersection you encounter when coming into town off Regional Road 8, the main road leading into town. (A six-way intersection split in the middle by a railroad crossing – and yet it was Lorne and Martindale in the city of Sudbury that earned the nickname *Killer's Crossing*).

But Levack didn't have one of those red, yellow, green lights. And Sudbury, that forty-five plus minute drive southeast, was the "big city" that regularly called to me when my young heart yearned for adventure.

Both, now, are an inclusive vision of what I think of when I think of "Home."

Yes, Levack, and Sudbury, continue to be true "Home" on my internal compass, despite calling cities like Ottawa, Hamilton, and Waterloo my home over the years.

Sean Costello was born in Ottawa and later moved to Sudbury where he spent most of his life working as an anesthesiologist prior to his retirement a few years ago.

Scott Overton was born in London, Ontario, later moved to Sudbury, and has been in the region for more than 30 years, 26 of which as a radio personality for *CIGM* and *Rewind 103.9*.

So, Sudbury is "Home" for all three of us.

And yes, I purposely spell "Home" with a capital letter. Because that's how important it feels.

When I think of my old stomping grounds – and, let's be honest, they are stomping grounds I return to multiple times a year, as my Mom still lives in Levack – I consider all of the positive influences to me as a person, but also as a writer.

I remember when Sean Costello's first novel **Eden's Eyes** came out in the late 1980s from Pocket Books. We learned that we had this "Stephen King of the North" in our midst.

Little did I know that, years later, when he was releasing his first venture into self-publishing, a dark humor thriller called **Finders Keepers**, and I met him in person for the first time at a book signing, that we would become friends, and he would become a mentor to me.

In fact, it wasn't long after that, back in 2004, when I was inspired by Sean into collecting a bunch of my previously published stories into a volume called **One Hand Screaming**. Leading me to create *Stark Publishing* an imprint I use for both publishing and my work within the book industry advising and coaching other writers.

Interestingly, it was the release of that first book that led me to meeting Scott Overton. Scott came out to my Thanksgiving weekend book launch at Chapters to interview me for the radio station where he worked. I learned that he was also a writer, and we struck up our friendship immediately.

My ongoing friendships and working relationships with both Scott and Sean have continued in various ways and on different levels.

Sean and I started collaborating on his own imprint, *Red Tower Publishing*, with me taking over the marketing and digital operations for his writing and publishing ventures, allowing him to focus on the writing. Similarly, it was Sean's prompt as a writing mentor that inspired me to turn a 10,000-word short story, "This Time Around" into a full-blown novel, **A Canadian Werewolf in New York**.

Speaking of which, Scott is the voice of Michael Andrews, the main character of that novel, as well as for the aforementioned short story and the next book in the series, **Stowe Away** which I recently released into audiobook format.

In addition, I had the honor of publishing both Sean and Scott in the 2012 anthology **Tesseracts Sixteen: Parnassus Unbound** for *Edge Science Fiction and Fantasy Publishing* out of Calgary, Alberta. Those two stories you will find reprinted on these pages.

As the person responsible for curating titles for the 2016 **Sudbury Ink: A Sudbury Writers' Guild Anthology**, I was pleased to present yet another story from Scott to the world.

I also had the pleasure of appearing in another anthology alongside Sean, in **Bluffs: Northeastern Ontario Stories from the Edge**. This was a book published by *Your Scrivener Press* led by Laurence Steven, retired professor of English from Laurentian University. Both of those stories also appear in the pages of this collection.

These are just some of the kinds of intricate and complex ties that we all have with Sudbury, and with one another.

I co-authored **Spooky Sudbury**, after all, with Jenny Jelen, years after leaving the community. Jenny and I met only because of her role as a journalist interviewing me about my first book of true ghost stories, **Haunted Hamilton**, was published. I knew her uncle in high school, but we became friends, and co-authors – and that experience led her to pursuing one of her own life-long passions for horseback riding.

That all came because of our mutual connection over that common home.

Because, in addition to folks like Sean and Scott, I can say that my dearest friends, people who will continue to be in my life, to inspire and move me, until the day that I die, are from Sudbury. Some have been with me from the time I was five years old; among the longest relationships I have ever had, and among the ones I cherish the most are, yes, all dear friends from my earliest days of growing up and going to school in Levack. Others I have had the good fortune to connect with later in life because we shared that common bond of "you're from Sudbury too?" that can instantly connect us with one another.

Like I said, there are intricate, complex, and deeply rooted connections and relationships we all have with one another and with the community that we consider our "Home" with a capital H.

Sudbury is not only in our blood, but it courses through our veins, is a part of the very breaths we inhale and exhale, the way that those deposits of nickel, gold, copper, and platinum, which slammed into the earth via a crashing meteorite some 1.8 million years ago enrich the very bedrock of the grounds that formed the Sudbury basin.

Something else that courses through our veins, besides this seemingly supernatural connection, is our penchant for exploring speculative tales: Stories that do not turn away from the shadows, but, instead, explore them, embrace them. Stories that consider science or the paranormal, and wonder "what if?"

Sean, Scott and I have long been drawn to consider such questions, and the answers appear in the prose that we create, as we pen tales of horror, of science fiction, or of just plain weird and eerie situations.

The stories you are about to read share some common themes with one another. Ghosts, or, at least, those unseen things that we can sometimes feel but which are ever present, is one common thread within them.

Our Home, or, if not that, then the elements of a place we all consider home, appear within these stories. Like the rich mineral deposits in the ground of the Sudbury basin, they might not be evident upon the surface, but upon closer inspection, I'm sure you'll realize they are there.

This is perhaps something for you to consider as you turn the page and enjoy the stories you are about to read. Or, maybe you can just ignore that, and enjoy reading some tales that will make you wonder, make you think, and perhaps leave you with a little bit of a chill; one that comes not from the impending fall season, but from the imaginative tales themselves.

Because, regardless of the content, topic, or situations that unfold in these stories you are about to read, and the creepy or eerie themes that bind them together, you'll also find some of the mysterious underlying foundation that continues to draw us in and keep us in Sudbury. Our Home.

- Mark Leslie Lefebvre
October 2020

SEAN COSTELLO

The Apology

Sean Costello

Originally appeared in Bluffs: Northeastern Ontario Stories from the Edge, *Edited by Laurence Steven, 2006.*

I guess being alone in this shoebox apartment was the worst. That and the awful restlessness of my late-night visitor. She was a big part of the reason I decided to battle the odds and apply for Jessica's adoption. It was a wild idea from the start. Thinking back, I can scarcely believe I dreamed it up. And even though it didn't work out exactly like I planned, I thank God I did what I did. I really thank God.

Jesse's here with me now, asleep in the spare bedroom. Tonight's her first night away from the hospital. Four long, loveless years in that place. It turns my heart cold to think of it. I can hear her raspy little snores from where I'm sitting. I guess I'll have to buy a humidifier for the poor thing. It's so dry in that back room.

The first time I saw Jesse was the day they brought her up to the children's ward. She was only six months old then. She looked so perfect, I fell in love with her right off: olive skin, tiny pink hands and feet, hair so blonde it was silver. And those blue, blue eyes. I still believe I'm the only one she's ever really looked at with those angel eyes. Most of the time they stay rolled up in their sockets, showing their underbellies.

It's a common thing at the chronic center, kids like Jesse, born without all of their faculties, left by their parents to die or just vegetate in one of those awful cage beds. That's what they kept Jesse in. It's like a crib, only the bars go right up over the top. Like a monkey cage, only not so roomy. She threw a lot of fits the first couple years; that was why they put her in the cage. She doesn't throw so many now, thank goodness, not since they got her medications squared away. They're godawful to witness, those fits. Her tiny body comes right off that rubber mattress, I swear, just like that kid in *The Exorcist*. She hisses and growls like that too, and her eyes flip way back in her head. One night she bit her tongue so hard they had to put three stitches in it. I was there that time, so the doctor let me hold her head while he sewed her up.

That's what scares me most about having her here, those damned fits. The nurses told me what to do, but it still scares me. Now that I have her, I believe I'd just die if I ever lost her.

Her natural mother was only a kid, sixteen or seven-teen at the most, so full of dope she couldn't even write her name on the release forms. It's a terrible thing to say, but little Jesse was probably better off on the ward than with that creature. But that's all behind her now, thank heaven, now that she's mine.

I work up at the chronic hospital, have since I was eighteen, almost twenty-seven years. It doesn't seem that long somehow. I quit for a while when things were good between Hal and me, and Hal was working steady. I was lucky they took me back when the bum started drinking again. Hal never did anything by half measures; once he found his stride, it only took him a couple years to drink himself to death. And good riddance.

I'm a cleaning lady up there, night shifts mostly. I'm in charge of the children's floor. The money isn't great, but it keeps the roof up and the belly warm. It's a job. What can a body expect with no high school or college degree? There'll be a little extra now that I've got my sweet Jesse. The Children's Aid promised a check regu-lar, every month. And my sister says she'll help out all she can. She'll be staying over, nights that I work. Dear Angie.

Like I said at the beginning, it was the visitor got me started on the idea. Mind, the first time I saw her I nearly jumped out of my skin. I never was one to believe in ghosts, that's for sure. But when you see one up close, face to face, well, the eye don't lie, my papa always said. Seeing is believing. Though I guess 'face to face' is the wrong phrase to use with this sorry little shade. You see, my ghost has no head.

It's small, a child I expect, a little girl, and it lives...can you say 'lives' when you're talking about a ghost? Anyway it 'stays' in the back of my bedroom closet. I was set to pick up and move the first couple times she appeared, but then I got curious. She meant me no harm, that much I could tell. And there was this terrible loneliness about her. I guess I felt sorry for her.

She only appears at night. I can tell when she's going to come because the room gets cold. Even in summer, when you suffer with the heat in these airless apartments, my skin goes all goosey just before she comes. One night—it was the middle of March, mind you, and cool down here anyway—I could actually see my breath when she popped out of the closet.

I had my sister over for a week after that one, so she could see it too. But it won't come out when I've got company, I know that now. (Angie searched the apartment for liquor one day when I was out doing groceries; I could tell. She thinks I'm crazy. Maybe she's right.)

It was when my visitor spoke the first time that I got the idea. I won't forget that night if I live to be a hundred. I swear, my windpipe nearly sealed over when I heard that terrible little voice. Why, there, my skin's gone goosey just thinking about it.

"I'm sorry, Mommy," she said, and Oh, God, there was pure terror in that voice. *"I'm so sorry."*

You might wonder how a thing with no head can speak. All I can tell you is I could hear the voice, but the sound was sort of on the inside, like a loud thought. That's the only way I can think to describe it.

After that, I decided to try and adopt Jessica. Like I said before, it was a crazy idea. But it was worth a shot, wasn't it? And even though I failed at one important part, isn't it better to have her here with me and out of that Godless place? I believe it is.

Despite the problems they said I'd have trying to adopt Jesse—I'm divorced, pushing fifty and living just this side of the poverty line, to list just a few—I think they gave her to me because they know I love her. Doctor Reed especially; I'm sure his good word really helped. I've almost lost my job a couple of times over Jesse, sitting with her, rocking her when I should've been doing the floors. Lord, how I used to rush through my work just to spend an hour with her before coming home to sleep the sunshine away. Sometimes, I honestly got the feeling she knew I was there. That she understood, felt my love. After all, real love is magical. She would cry when I put her back in that cage. Not cry...she doesn't cry in the way we think of it. It's a kind of animal sound, lowing. It breaks your heart, believe me.

The wild, really nutty part of my plan was this: I figured if I could trap my little ghost somehow, then maybe, just maybe, I could get her into Jesse. Get her to be the child's soul. When you look at Jess, you don't need an education to see the poor thing has no soul. And she's so perfect otherwise, her body I mean, not all twisted like so many of the others up there. When I told Angie about the idea, she sort of backed away and said, "Tabby, you watch too much TV." That's probably true. I'm sure I never would've thought of it if I hadn't seen some of those shows, you know, those horror shows, that sci-fi stuff. When you're alone you watch a lot of TV.

The kicker was how to catch her.

Thinking about it got me wondering how she died. I thought of asking the landlord about previous tenants, but he's a scabby old lech who keeps telling me he's got a thing for chubby women. Well, this is one chubby woman he'll never get his feelers into. Not a chance.

I took a trip to the public library and waded through a bunch of microfilmed newspapers—a child murder in a town like Sudbury would make big news—but no luck there. I gave that up for a bad habit when I started seeing double. Then I did ask a few questions: the police, the neighbors. But nobody knew anything. Or if they did, they were keeping it to themselves.

Still, it was hard not to wonder. Seeing as this ghost had no head, some pretty gruesome possibilities came to mind. I never had any children, but even so, it's hard to imagine harming one, let alone committing murder. The wondering started to work its way into my sleep. There, in the nightmare, the imagination runs wild.

How do you catch a ghost? I couldn't come up with a single idea. I did notice one thing about her, though, something I thought I could use. When she appears—and she's always wearing that same powder blue skirt and white ruffled blouse—it seems she can't just pass through things, the way you'd expect a ghost could. Once, she bumped into the bureau, and even though I could see right through her, she didn't just blend into it. She turned away from it. The only place she vanishes is inside the closet. One time I tried to get past her, to shut the closet door, but she got frightened and rushed back inside. Another time I rigged a crude sort of pulley affair, so I could close the door from my bed. But she wouldn't come out, not until I took the pulley away. It was like she knew.

Then it came to me.

And to my mind, at the time anyway, it seemed like a foolproof plan. Once I was set up, though, it took nearly a week for her to appear.

But last night she came.

And I *caught* her.

I don't mind saying, by the time last night rolled around, I was getting pretty discouraged. I figured if I didn't nab her soon I never would, since Jesse was coming home today and that little spook refuses to come out when I'm not alone. It was my last chance. So I decided to sit up all night and watch for her. God knows, I might've slept through all kinds of her blind wanderings in the ten years I've been a tenant here and never even known.

I sat in bed against a heap of pillows, a pot of coffee on the nightstand beside me. I tried to read, but by half-past three the coffee pot was empty and my eyes were heavy with sleep. I kept nodding off. Between shifts like that, it's hard to get back on a normal person's schedule. Sometimes I can sit up late with the TV, but I didn't want to use it for fear of scaring her off with the noise.

Just before dawn, that frightful, pleading voice cut me like a razor.

"I'm sorry, Mommy...so sorry..."

I was right off to sleep before that, still propped against the headboard. When I opened my eyes, she was standing right beside me, not two feet away, those tiny arms outstretched like she wanted me to pick her up and give her a hug.

When I popped up and reached for the Electrolux I'd left by the bed, her arms came smartly down by her sides, her hands balled into fists, and she started making a terrible animal sound, like what Jesse used to do when I put her back in her cage.

For the first time since the start, I was terrified of my little spook. Not of what she might do to me so much. No. It was more what she stood for that got inside me like a dead thing, the empty place she came from, the senseless violence that must have put her there.

The vacuum was already plugged in, the bag inside brand new. I grabbed the flexible hose, hit the power button, and aimed the nozzle right at her. She took a clumsy step toward the closet, but the suction already had her. In a wink, she vanished through that nozzle like a discarded bit of cloth. I left the power on until I had the machine open and my hand over the mouth of the bag, then I slapped a square of duct tape over the opening.

I had her.

I dressed in a panic. Amazing what you don't think of in advance; if I'd had my wits about me, I would've left my street clothes on. I kept the vacuum bag beside me the whole time, talking to it, reassuring it. Then I called a cab and had the driver take me up to the hospital. I bet he had a story to tell over coffee at the end of his shift, a fat lady whispering to a vacuum bag.

I guess I never believed I'd catch her, not really, because there was one important part of the plan I hadn't considered: now that I had her, how was I supposed to get her to take up lodgings inside my sweet Jessica? My mother called me an idiot once; I don't think once was enough. Going up to level five on the elevator, I decided I'd just have to play it by ear.

There was grey morning light sifting through the blinds by the time I got to Jesse. She was lying on her side with her back tight to the bars, her tiny wrists all red from tugging at those godforsaken restraints. Her eyes were rolled back, like usual, and the poor thing was drooling. Somewhere on the other side of the ward a child was crying, the most mournful sound you'd ever want to hear. And all of a sudden, I couldn't wait to get Jesse as far away from there as my meager savings would allow. Right then, I didn't even care if my little scheme worked or it didn't. I just wanted us out of there.

I'm glad none of the nurses happened by when I was doing this, because they might've reported me as crazy and I'd've lost Jesse before I even had her. I wasn't supposed to pick her up until ten.

I set the vacuum bag on a chair and lifted Jesse out of her cage. I sat with her awhile, rocking her, the bag wedged between her heart and mine. And I swear that bag felt cold, like it had some frozen food inside.

I talked to Jesse, talked to the bag, rocked, prayed. Then, around eight-thirty, I decided I'd just have to gamble. I stuck the hole in front of Jesse's little mouth, ripped off the tape, and gave the bag a squeeze.

Nothing came out. And Jesse didn't change.

I should've known.

I cried some, tossed the bag in the waste bin, then joined the day girls for coffee. They brought my spirits up some. At ten, I collected my baby and cabbed home.

Like I said, it was a crazy idea.

*   *   *

"I'm sorry, Mommy...so sorry..."

I dropped the magazine I was reading and pushed away from the table, that voice getting right inside me. I thought at the very least I'd gotten rid of my ghost.

But it was back.

And it was in my baby's room.

I rushed to the bedroom door and swung it open, fearful of what the spirit might do, afraid I'd angered it, harmed it in some way, and now it meant to avenge itself on Jessica.

I stood at the foot of the single bed in shock. It took me a moment to move again, and when I did I had to feel my way through a blur of tears.

Jesse was sitting up in the middle of the bed, all by herself. Her clear blue eyes were wide open, tear-filled and fixed on mine, and her tiny, perfect arms were outstretched, as if she wanted to be picked up and hugged.

"I'm sorry, Mommy..." she said again, fear making her new voice tremble, "...so sorry."

I scooped her into my loving arms. "It's okay, my angel," I whispered. "Hush. There's nothing to be sorry about. Nothing at all."

Writer's Block

Sean Costello

Originally appeared in Tesseracts Sixteen: Parnassus Unbound, *Edited by Mark Leslie, 2012.*

Aw shit!"

Darrin Keene hammered the backspace key, tucked a strip of Taperaser over the typo, and struck the error into oblivion. Now he hit the proper key, completing the word. He reread the short paragraph he'd been laboring over for the past half-hour.

The night was a page torn from an arctic explorer's diary, the last page, unfinished, a page left rasping in the wind next to his frozen body. A cutting northerly rattled the panes, howling through the eaves like a starving she-wolf. Snow smothered everything beneath its crippling weight. Beyond the cabin, the ice-sheeted lake

creaked and groaned. It was a bleak night, a night
through which nothing warm could endure.

"Starving she-wolf," Darrin said, shaking his head at the overkill.

But it *was* that kind of night. Even his weighty verbiage fell short of describing it. It was the dead of February, and the storm beyond the single-pane windows was fierce and unrelenting.

Darrin had rented this isolated cabin in the Kukagami wilderness for exactly that reason. The setting. What better backdrop for an aspiring horror novelist to work against? What richer font of inspiration?

But Jesus, he thought, *what a shit-kicker of a storm.* It seemed to distract more than inspire him.

He pushed his chair back from the old Underwood and moved to the stone hearth, the fire dwindling to coals now. The wood-frame cabin was poorly insulated and a bitch to heat (*she-bitch* he thought, grinning). He lay a length of birch on the coals and leaned closer, spreading his numb fingers as the papery bark crackled into yellow flame.

It was eight o'clock and dark as pitch. Darrin had by now given up hope of Shelley arriving tonight, and his sense of longing, developed over the course of a lonesome week up here, flared like the bark in the fire. He'd spent the past two days thinking of little else but the voluptuous curves and valleys of Shelley's body, spread out hot and willing on the sheepskin rug in front of the fire-place. He could almost see her there now, in the pixie dance of flames.

Ah, Shelley. Warm, mammoth-breasted Shelley.

The image vanished as another took its place—Shelley stranded and freezing in a broken-down Honda Civic, halfway up that godforsaken road from the highway. He prayed she hadn't ventured out in this hell-hole of a night. And he realized then, in that instant of terrible possibility, he loved Shelley. It really was more than the out-of-this-world humping they managed together. Somewhere along the line, he'd truly begun to love her.

But Shelley was no dummy. She'd never drive on a night like this. She'd grown up in the North, had heard enough of the real-life horror stories to know better.

Darrin stood awhile longer, soaking up the warmth of the fire, then returned to the Underwood. From somewhere outside came the mournful cry of a real wolf, and Darrin's hackles bristled. He hit the tab key and began a new paragraph.

> *But the cold thing, the bloodless creature conceived in some deep and stinking cave where even God could not see, was unbothered by the storm. The shrieking wind aroused It, beckoned It. It rose from the muck of the lake bed and thrust a twisted claw up through three feet of ice. The winter air instantly froze the water layering Its scales; but Its taloned digits flexed and shed the icy crust like an exoskeleton.*

A tortured groan rose from the ice as it cracked once more from beneath. A second limb poked through into the air. And now a third.

Darrin smirked, excited by the dank menace he was creating. He loved monster stories, had since childhood: Frankenstein, The Werewolf, The Blob, countless others. He knew that credible horror tales, things that could actually happen, had a wider appeal, were more marketable. But the monster stories, usually short, he penned for an audience of one: himself. He secured them like treasures in a special section of his filing cabinet, pulling them out when the light was low and the mood macabre. If he ever got famous, he'd assemble them into an anthology: *Miscreations*, by Darrin Keene.

He got up, paced the room, tried to visualize the shit-encrusted aberration that had thus far punched three scaly appendages through three feet of ice. How in hell did you come up with a monster someone else hadn't already conceived? Or did it even matter what the mindless flesh-eater looked like, as long as it left a trail of gore?

He moved to the picture window now, overlooking the lake. And as he watched the twists and swirls of wind-whipped snow, he heard the eerie moan and faint thunder of the ice shifting on the lake. It sure as hell was a creepy sound. The lake was huge and deep, dotted here and there with rocky islands. The gale-force winds had blown its surface clean; now, it looked like a sprawling black hole in the midst of blue desert dunes.

Again he returned to the typewriter, sat, reread the few scant lines. Then stared at the keys, his mind a blank. . How would this bit of aquatic pestilence look? He simply couldn't conjure an image. And he believed he knew why. Tonight, right now, he should've been tangled on the sheepskin rug with Shelley the Amazon woman, Shelley the ravenous she-wolf. Humping. Like animals.

Shit.

It was more than that, though. There was still this diffuse worry that maybe she *had* set out to drive up here. If that were the case, she should've arrived hours ago. He couldn't bear the thought of her marooned in this storm. A dull sense of helplessness nagged him. He was totally isolated up here, had *chosen* to be isolated, couldn't even pick up one of Ma Bell's little miracle machines and dial the seven simple digits that would put his mind at ease.

But it was more even than that. It was this freaking blizzard. The storm was giving him the willies. It was so cold. He couldn't imagine a place colder, more lifeless and desolate, than the endless sprawl of hills and fir trees beyond this cabin. If a man got lost out there, it was game over. February in Northern Ontario. Absolute-fucking-zero.

Life-forms…none.

Except one, he thought, shivering. *Me.*

Now *there* was something to consider. That whoring wind licking down the chimney, trying to snuff out the fire; the very real possibility he could freeze to death up here.

He hit the tab key.

No ideas.

Then it dawned. He reached into his knapsack and pulled out a joint. He'd almost forgotten this little muther. It had been intended for him and Shelley; she really got off sexually when she was high. Which meant he did, too.

Damn.

He struck a wood match on the side of the typewriter and lit up. A gift from his dad, this old Underwood. Manual. No electricity up here anyway. Typing by oil lamp.

Darrin filled his lungs, stifling the urge to cough, then exhaled an aromatic plume. Pink Kush, the dealer had called it, from Jamaica.

He took another hit, his anxiety already abating.

And outside, the wind squalled.

There was a dreadful crash behind him now and Darrin lurched to his feet, dropping the joint, knocking the press-back chair to the floor in a clatter of wood against wood. He pivoted, bringing his fists up in a defensive reflex.

Snow billowed along the hallway from the front door. Flames crackled in the hearth, thinning as if to extinguish. The storm was in the living room.

Darrin lurched into the hall, chilled to the marrow. For an eager moment, he thought it might be Shelley, arrived after all. But it had been the wind, kicking the door open with all the force of a battering ram. He caught a glimpse of the blue-white hump that was his snow-covered Jeep as he shoved the door tight to its frame. He threw the iron bolt and leaned against the door, looking with a sort of wonder at the dusting of snow in the hallway; diamonds glittering in lamp light.

He was feeling the dope.

He had a sudden, desperate longing for Shelley.

The cabin creaked, wind lashed the pines. For a wild moment, he considered pulling on his parka, digging out the Jeep and taking his chances.

But no, that would be suicide.

He went back to the Underwood.

> *Even in the harsh blizzard air, It stank of ooze and rot. Its single, misshapen eye found the yellow rectangle of light that was the picture window, and was drawn to it. The gob of putrid protoplasm that functioned as Its brain, a malign nerve centre knowing only hunger, propelled the beast forward, up the snow-crusted incline toward that warm yellow spill.*

""Okay," Darrin said aloud, pleased. He retrieved the fallen joint and relit it. "*Now* this sucker's coming to life. Oh mama, I can almost smell It." He filled his lungs and exhaled, filled and exhaled. Already he could feel the weed heightening his imagination.

Time for a scene change.

He took a last lingering toke, then pinched off the ember. Sparks tumbled to the rough-hewn floor and Darrin stamped them under his boot. He thought of Shelley and sheepskin, then started typing, two-finger, fast.

Doug Hamilton lay naked before the fire, sipping champagne, watching Sharon as she slipped out of scant undergarments. Her skin was dark, her eyes a rich moss-green, her lips full and moist. She moved with slow, erotic grace, turning, bending, giving her man a languishing view of all her lovely parts. Now she draped herself over him, tenting his face with her luxurious, jet black mane, brushing his lips with kisses like velvet. He put his champagne aside but the glass tipped, sending amber fingerlets bubbling over the rustic wood floor.

The cabin belonged to Doug's brother. And Doug had it for the next six days, the cabin and Sharon and miles of idyllic isolation. Even the storm seemed perfect for their first night alone. It drew them closer, intensified the hearth-side warmth of the place.

Darrin paused, slapping his hands together with malicious delight. "Got it up yet, Douglas?" he said to the typed page. "I hope so, because pretty soon, 'It' is gonna rip it right off for you." He cackled. He was ripped. His stomach growled. His mouth was parched, his eyelids leaden. He grabbed the box of Frito's off the table by the Underwood and dug in.

Munchies, Manfred.

Now he looked at the page, deciding whether or not to allow Doug Hamilton his nooky before becoming an hors-d'oeuvre for a mutant. He considered constructing a full page of gruesomely detailed hardcore horror; even worse, he weighed the possibilities of Sharon and the thing—catchy title—*Sex Slave of the Mud Lake Mutant*.

"Whoa, boy," he said to his reflection in the window. "You're decompensating now. You got a good little monster tale going here. Don't screw it up."

He wiped his fingers on his jeans and typed, deciding he'd make the cabin in the story identical to the one he was in (except warmer), recalling what a wise old English prof had told him: *Write what you know*. And he wanted to use the door banging open in the wind; that had been suitably freaky. That would be how the eating-machine got in. Then it would creep, or maybe ooze, into the kitchen, hide around the corner while Doug went back to the fireplace...

A deliberate scratching sound made Darrin turn on his chair.

"Who's there?"

The words hung on the chill cabin air. The scratching came again, on the apex of a powerful gust, and Darrin saw the branches of a nearby tree scraping the north window.

"Paranoid," he mumbled. "Par-a-*noid*."

He thought about the scaly Mud Lake Mutant. And typed.

> *The cabin door swung open with a nerve-jangling crash, making the lovers yelp in fear. Snow billowed into the room on sub-zero gusts.*

*"The damn door blew open," Doug said, an-
noyed and at the same time relieved to have a
simple explanation for the startling intrusion. He
grabbed his housecoat and pulled it on, noticing
the spilled champagne and the oddly crimson hue
it had created on the floorboards. That it looked
like a pool of blood chilled him in a manner distinct from that caused by the bracing air. Just an
illusion of color caused by the reflection of the
fire, he decided, and started along the hall to the
door. His knees and ankles burned in the glacial
wind.*

*Sharon curled closer to the fire. The fright had
destroyed her mood.*

*Doug pushed the door shut, fired the heavy bolt
and cursed under his breath. The keen pitch of
arousal he'd been reaching had evaporated. He
knew it would be the same for Sharon.*

*He noticed the odor first, like fish gone over.
Then, as he stepped around the patina of snow in
the hallway, he noticed something else, beneath
his bare feet: an icy, gelatinous film, like the goo
on refrigerated turkey.*

What the hell . . .?

*The sound came next, a boggy slithering punc-
tuated by stertorous breathing . . .*

Darrin paused. There was an abrupt lull in the wind,
and that bothered him. Because the scratching sound was

there again. Only now, in this freak quiet, it seemed to be coming from *inside* the cabin. From the kitchen.

His breath quickened. He rose off the chair, remaining in a tense crouch. He grabbed a length of birch off the wood pile, liking its heft.

"Shelley?"

No answer. Of course. He'd bolted the door from the inside.

The wind held its curious silence, as if waiting. In the distance, the wolf howled its haunting cry. Birch, blackened and glowing, crackled in the fireplace.

Darrin tiptoed toward the kitchen, holding his breath. Floorboards creaked under his weight, the sound amplified in the eerie calm. It was as if some celestial film crew had switched off the machinery of a simulated blizzard: *Scene change, next night, dead silence, cry of lone wolf.*

Darrin edged around the corner into the kitchen, brandishing the birch log.

The kitchen was empty.

He sighed, saying, "Rodents. Varmints."

But now he caught a whiff of rot. Ridiculously, he looked at the wood floor. For turkey goo. There was none.

Of course.

But what was that rancid smell?

He opened the cooler containing his provisions: only fresh scents from in there. This was the reek of something long dead. He wondered why he hadn't noticed it before now. Maybe there *had* been a rodent—a field mouse maybe, frozen to death in some dark corner of the cabin in December or January—that had begun to rot over the course of the week he'd been heating the place.

He opened the cupboard under the sink, rooted around, found nothing, shrugged. He continued through the kitchen, then along the hallway to the main room.

His eye caught movement now, something so fleeting it could have been a hallucination; he prayed it *had* been. He noticed it as he stepped out of the hallway, something black and glistening, snake-like, whipping around the corner into the south section of the cabin where the Underwood sat on a makeshift desk.

Darrin wished he hadn't smoked that reefer.

He waited, listening. The wind had resumed its former pitch, and Darrin welcomed that now; it blocked the smaller cabin noises that were freaking him out of his woollies. He wondered what the guy he'd bought the weed from had laced it with. He knew all kinds of illicit shit could turn up in a bag of weed, just to give it that extra kick: horse tranquilizer, low-grade smack. There must've been *something* in it, because he didn't usually hallucinate on grass.

Hallucination, right?

Crouching now, frightened, he moved to the next corner, peered along the adjoining wall. Nothing there.

Okay.

He straightened.

But what if it had slithered around the *next* corner, back into the kitchen? He checked the floorboards again; they were dry, unsoiled.

What if . . .?

Are you going whacko, Keene? Forget it. Write!

A noise. In the kitchen. Scraping.

"Shelley?" he asked the emptiness. "If that's you screwing around, I'll—" He remembered the bolted door. Unless she—or something—had gotten in when the door blew open.

"Jesus," he said in a whisper, "what would Doug Hamilton do right now?"

Go and look. What else?

He crept back to the kitchen. Bugger-all there. Now he inched through the room to the hallway. *Nothing.* He moved quickly to the next corner, almost running. *Zip.* Then, brandishing the log and whooping like a wild man, he bolted around the entire cabin, twice, using the barnwood corners as pivots, boots thudding the floorboards.

Halfway around the third time, he stopped by the Underwood and leaned on the desk, breathless, feeling like an idiot. A dog chasing its tail. But now he understood how Doug Hamilton would be feeling, and wanted to get it into words while it was still fresh. Coming clear too, was a mental picture of his imaginary Mud Lake Monster. He took a final glance behind him—just to be sure—then sat at the typewriter, scrolled the page up on the carriage, and reread the last sentence.

> *The sound came next, a boggy slithering punctuated by stertorous breathing . . .*

And now Darrin heard it.

Plain as day.

Something foul, frigid, and inhumanly powerful, took hold of Darrin Keene's head and twisted. Darrin caught a glimpse of It before the oil lamp extinguished.

Oddly, his last thought as he looked up was: *That's It!*

* * *

On the afternoon of the next day, Shelley England followed a big yellow snow plow up Kukagami Road toward the cabin. The plow operator was her second cousin, Brad Thomson, and although he wasn't supposed to, Brad veered off the main road and cleared out the three hundred yards of track leading in to the cabin. As Brad reversed the machine to leave, Shelley gave him a toothy grin that made him wish for the millionth time since grade school that Shelley E. hadn't been born his cousin.

Shelley parked the Civic behind the snowy hump of Darrin's Jeep. She was surprised to see the cabin door ajar. But the day was sunny and mild, as so often happened up here after a storm, and she guessed he was airing the place out. It surprised her too that he hadn't come out when the plow lumbered into the yard. Maybe he was out on the racks, catching the rays.

But now she noticed there were no footprints outside the cabin, and a vague worry came over her. Haltingly, she approached the open door.

The storm had raged for thirty-six hours, snow drifting most of the way up the north wall of the cabin; the windows on that side were completely covered. Inside, the hallway was darkly shadowed.

Shelley stepped in. "Darrin?"

Her worry vanished when she realized he was probably just hiding on her. Darrin was a prankster. Shelley liked that about him; always a good time. But she hated being scared. Darrin loved to sneak up and goose his victims.

"Darrin? Talk to me. If you frighten me..."

She approached the kitchen with her back to the wall. The smell of rotten fish was abrupt and powerful.

"Darrin? What have you been eating up here?"

She rounded the corner, irritated now with his silence. That was when she saw the press-back chair lying on the floor in front of the Underwood.

She screamed when she saw congealed blood tracking across the typewriter keys, and up onto the unfinished page.

*   *   *

The forensics team verified the blood type as Darrin's. The police found no footprints in the snow, but did notice the large, healed-over rent in the ice. When Shelley beseeched them to send in divers, they refused, saying it was too dangerous this time of year. They thought the hole in the ice was too large to have been made by a man anyway. When pressed for an alternate explanation, they could provide none. They told her if

Darrin had in fact gone through the ice, there was nothing to do but wait until spring. Then, they said, his body would likely turn up in the thaw.

But it never did.

MARK LESLIE

Being Needed

Mark Leslie

Originally appeared in Bluffs: Northeastern Ontario Stories from the Edge, *Edited by Laurence Steven, 2006.*

Grandpa had acted strangely the last couple of times I'd visited him at the nursing home. Normally, getting a story out of him was easy — telling tales had always been as natural as breathing to him. Grandpa loved talking, spinning words, having an audience, even an audience of one. But lately, he'd been more quiet than normal. There seemed be something beneath the surface.

It was only after a lot of prodding that I was able to get him to tell me what it was.

"Okay, okay, Peter, I'll tell you." Grandpa paused in mid thought to take a drag on his unlit pipe. "But except for Bill Johnson, you're the only person who'll know about this; and since that ol' fart don't remember his own goddamn name half the time, it'll probably be our little secret. In fact," he looked me squarely in the eyes, "it better be."

Over the years Grandpa's stories had often been outrageous, especially the fishing tales, but that day I could tell by the furtive look in his eyes that the story I was going to hear would be different.

It was my usual Friday after work ritual to share with Grandpa the excitement of my eight-month-old daughter and the successes of my career. A few observant co-workers had suggested that my clockwork visits indicated some guilt for allowing him to live in a nursing home. But it wasn't entirely guilt that drove me to visit Grandpa. Sure, when the home first became necessary, I felt bad about it and used to visit with the old man at least two or three times a week, which in retrospect does seem like a lot. But I'd enjoyed those visits, and initially my wife had been fully supportive. After all, me visiting with my Grandfather was certainly a better option than having him come live with us. But after a while, she started to see my multiple visits as a bit obsessive. And once our daughter was born, she put a stop to more than a single weekly visit, reminding me that my priorities shouldn't be stretching back a couple of generations, but should focus on my immediate family.

Well, she was right. So while I'll admit that my regular visits with Grandpa were driven by a degree of guilt, I also looked forward to hearing him spin tales, just like when I was a kid and would ride my bike across town on

Friday afternoons to share in a glass of iced tea and one of Grandpa's monologues.

But that day the tale would be different. He pursed his lips against the stem of the unlit pipe, then pushed his wire frame glasses up the bridge of his nose.

"You might think, Peter, that an old bugger like me woulda lost his marbles by now. You might think that after hearing what I'm about to tell you. So, think what you want. I know that I got all my marbles in all the right places—and that's all that really matters.

"Now you know Mr. Johnson, I know you do. He's a fine man, but dumb as a board sometimes. Well, old Johnson and me, we were sitting in the day room playing cribbage at a table near the window. I remember it was near the window because it was late August and Fern Sampson kept yelling at us to close the window, he was freezin' his poor old eggs off. Johnson just sat there, his long white beard ruffling in the wind, deaf to anything that wasn't half in his ear already, and I just plain ignored the old grump. It wouldn't be long before the winter, when you couldn't afford to open any windows without pneumonia killing half the people living here. Yeah, it was late August of this year when Johnson and me were enjoying a cribbage game and Mrs. Crampton walked in and stirred things up.

"'Carl,' she said to me. 'I need to talk to you.'

"Norma was a fine girl. You could tell that she had been a real looker in her day. She had probably broken a lot of hearts once upon a time, but her face had since been sculpted by years of loneliness. One of the sad things about this place, Peter, is that we're all of an age where we just may not wake up tomorrow. The only thing you can depend on here is losing your friends; it's the only constant, and you have to deal with it again and again. That summer, Norma had lost three of her closest friends within two weeks, and I guess she was afraid of getting close to anyone anymore. Certainly, by that time she had very few friends left that she could lose.

"'Sit yourself down, dear.' I said to her. 'We'll have a little talk.'

"'What?' Johnson shouted.

"'Nothing." I said to him, then turned back to her. "What is it, Norma?'

"'Well, Carl, for the past few weeks I've been hearing something in the middle of the night. Something I haven't heard for what seems like an eternity. I can't block it from my mind, and I don't think I can deal with it anymore.'

"I put down my cards and looked at her. You know, it's a shame to see someone losing it after all the years they've put into making a good life, and I was about ready to believe the poor old dear had gone batty—probably like you're gonna think about me when this story's over. So, after just looking at her silently, I asked, 'What kind of things are you hearing, Norma?'

"'I can hear a baby crying.'

"'Is that it? There's nothing strange about hearing that, Norma. If your window is open, you can hear noises from clear across the city. And a baby's cry, well that's a piercing noise, that is.'

"I laid my hand down on hers and could feel her shaking. So I got up to close the window.

"'That house there Carl, that one across the laneway. Do you see it?'"

I followed Grandpa's glance out his bedroom window and knew that despite its not being visible from this side of the building, in his mind's eye he was seeing a brick and stucco two-story with a veranda, just beginning to be shadowed by early evening.

That house.

I braced myself for what was coming.

"I stood looking at the window, and there was that same old house that just stares back with blank haunting eyes. You know it Peter, after what happened there. It's a nice big old house, built back when house building was a distinct art, not just a cookie cutter neighborhood crammed together and put up over a couple of weeks. And you know it used to be a nice looking house earlier this summer. The young family that moved in in the late spring—watching them unpacking had given us all something to do. You could tell that they were just starting out. Good lookin' couple, but young, you remember."

I did. Grandpa and I had spent a couple of Friday visits speculating on where they got the money to buy the big house, but they seemed friendly, always smiling and laughing and kissing each other.

After a couple months or so, though, the loveliness turned into a nightmare. Instead of the usual morning scene of the young man kissing his wife and baby goodbye on the porch steps, one day in early August, Grandpa and the other residents had woken to see a mess of police cars and ambulances parked outside. Apparently, for some unknown reason, in the middle of the night the man had carved his wife's body into small pieces while she slept. Then he'd used the knife to open his own throat. They'd found both bodies in the upstairs bedroom, but the baby was never found. One of the rumors was that the man had killed the baby and perhaps carved it up and flushed it down the toilet, but no evidence could ever prove that theory.

I have to admit that I stopped listening to Grandpa's story for a moment as my mind replayed the gruesome details. My wife and I had done our best to erase the memory of this event. Especially since that family next door and our own seemed to share such similar circum-stances. Young, starting out, a new baby in the house. And I knew how tough it could be. Before my daughter turned three months old, my wife and I had been walking zombies, living on less than three or four hours of sleep a day. But I failed to understand how that man could have turned on his wife and child and murdered them in cold blood. The mere thought of it sent a cold shiver down my spine. I struggled to focus again on Grandpa's story.

"...and I wondered what could have happened to that nice young couple to turn their world so suddenly into tragedy.

"'Yeah, Norma, I know the house.'

"'That's where the crying is coming from.'

"She had a look in her eyes, Peter, of what some might call conviction. And I wanted to believe her. I did. But I explained to her that nobody lived there.

"She refused to take that for an answer, grabbed my hand in hers and said, 'Surely you remember the fact that they couldn't find the baby's body.'

"'Well, yes,' I'd said.

"'My window faced the house. I used to watch the mother feed that baby on the porch in the warmth of the afternoon sun. I watched that family with as much passion and love as I felt for my own children, my own grandchildren, who have since mostly abandoned me. I looked forward to each day because of that family; I'd follow their daily activities. I lived to see what they were doing. When it all went bad, a part of me died, Carl. Don't you see?'

"'I understand, Norma, I do.'

"'I don't think you really do, Carl. When that man murdered his family, I felt alone again. As alone as when my own family first deposited me here. But I now know that I'm not truly alone. That baby, the one whose body had not been found, is calling out to me.'

"She insisted that a few days after the couple had died, she started hearing this crying in the middle of the night. I told her it wasn't possible, that it must be her imagination. She fretted for a moment then stopped and gave me a strange look, lifted her index finger as if to make a point, then turned and left."

Grandpa paused, looked off for a moment, chewed on the stem of his pipe, then looked at me without saying anything. It was obvious he was thinking about something and deciding whether or not he was going to tell me.

"I didn't see her again until late that night. I was awakened from sleep to find a figure standing in the doorway.

"'Johnson,' I growled. 'You old fart. You're sleepwalking. Go back to bed.'

"'Carl.' It was a woman's voice. Norma.

"'Yeah?'

"'Come with me.'

"I dragged my legs over the side of the bed. 'What the hell?'

"'I can hear the crying, Carl. I can hear it again.'

"'Norma. Jesus, woman. It's two in the morning.'

"'You didn't believe me. But I need you to believe me, Carl. I need someone to believe. And I know you will once you hear it. So come with me, to hear it.'

"I grabbed my housecoat and smirked at Johnson on the way out. The old bugger slept through the whole conversation. A tank could have run down the middle of the room and he wouldn't have heard it.

"I followed Norma to her room. I sat on the bed and Norma went to the window. From the moonlight I could see the hint of tears welling in her eyes.

"'Norma, I can't...' I began.

"'Shh...listen.'

"We sat in the dark a few moments, staring at each other, and then it finally came to my ears. My eyes must have widened, showing her what she was looking for. Her face broke into a tearful smile as she looked back at me. I heard it all right. Clear as a bell. The steady wailing of a child that wakes in the night, wanting to be fed or changed. It was a baby, no doubt about that.

"We listened for a few moments. Occasionally, the baby would stop to take a few breaths and then it would start all over again. I don't know how long we sat there listening to it, but the next thing I remember is Norma standing in front of me with tears just rolling down her face.

"'Carl, it's driving me mad. There's a baby in that house. And it needs me.'

"'It can't be coming from the house, Norma.' I said. But all the while I realized there was no other place it could be coming from to sound so close and clear.

"'It is Carl. That baby needs me.'

"I swallowed noisily, my throat suddenly dry.

"'I'm going to it, Carl,' she said, walking over to look out the window at the house again. 'I'm going to make that crying stop.'

"At that moment an attendant came into the room, wondering what we were up to and saying we were making enough noise to wake Old Johnson—which, around here, is the equivalent to waking the dead. He calmed Norma into bed and then ushered me back to my room.

"When I settled back into bed, Peter, I swear I thought I could still hear that baby crying. I know it's impossible, but it was as if that baby was crying right outside my bedroom door. I even got up, twice, to check, but when I stuck my head out into the corridor, the crying seemed to be coming from the direction of Norma's room.

"The second time I stuck my head out, I decided to follow the noise toward its source. It was funny, now that I think of it, that the attendant hadn't commented on the sound of a baby crying so loudly.

"When I got to Norma's door, it was open a crack, so I slipped in quickly, afraid that the attendant might find me in the hall. The crying was louder inside Norma's room and I just stood there, letting it pierce my mind.

"A moment later, when my eyes had adjusted to the darkness, I discovered Norma wasn't in the room. She was gone. As I stood in that empty room I was overtaken by a totally unexpected wave of loneliness. I went to the window and looked at the house, and I didn't have my glasses on, so I can't be sure of what I saw, but I can tell you I did see something.

"A woman I believe to be Norma Crampton was going up the porch steps to the house. I strained my eyes, and watched the blurry figure open the door and go in as if it wasn't even locked, never mind boarded over.

"I stood at the window, listening to the crying—mesmerized by it—when all of a sudden it stopped. It just plain stopped. And the silence that followed was like nothing I've ever heard—or not heard. The crying had stopped, and I knew why.

"I left Norma's room and went straight to my bed. It never entered my head to call the attendants. Imitating Johnson, I pulled the covers over my head and spent the rest of the night trying to sort out my emotions—incredulity from conviction, a rising terror from a growing sense of peace. I think, finally, I was envious of Norma. Of the fact that she had found a calling and answered it.

"The next day, everyone was aware that Norma was missing. I was asked about her, since the attendant remembered that she and I had been together that night. And I told them that she must have decided to leave because she couldn't stand the loneliness anymore. I told them that was what we'd been talking about that night, but I didn't have a chance to convince her otherwise because I'd been escorted back to my room.

"They believed me. You'd be surprised how many old people just get up and walk out of places like this, never to be seen again. And you know, what I told them was the truth. It was what happened—she did leave because of loneliness. So I wasn't really lying when I said that. I never told anyone about the crying or about what I thought I saw through the window that night, until now."

I sat back, letting my legs slip back down to the floor, momentarily thinking about how easily I could stiffen up now when sitting in that manner. Grandpa took another imaginary puff from his pipe while I rubbed my legs and waited for him to sum up his tale.

"You see, Peter, old people can get lonely. They can long for the days when there was someone to look after. Whatever happened that night—whatever really happened—I'll never truly know. But I do know one thing. I know that Norma made that baby stop crying. I don't know where she is now, or what happened to that baby, but she made the crying stop.

"And in a sense, that baby made Norma's crying stop. No, she wasn't crying in any physical sense. But her soul was crying. Like I said, an old person can get really lonely. But Norma had been needed, or had thought she had been needed by another being—and that was worth the world to her.

"One last thing, Peter. I've told you this story because I trust you. But you can't tell anyone about it."

"Of course, I won't Grandpa."

"I mean, anyone."

"Nobody."

"I don't want anybody to think I've lost my marbles, after all," he added, with a smile that looked a bit forced.

I left the nursing home that day feeling disturbed. Of all the tales my Grandfather had spun over the years, even among the fishing tales, never had he told such a whopper and tried so convincingly to pass it off as the truth. Of course, it had to be a whopper, but the earnest way he spoke of Norma and the baby, and loneliness, left me worried about him, and feeling guilty at leaving him by himself in that place.

When I got home that night it was a relief to see my wife and baby. I held them close and told them that I'd had a great day at work and, honoring my promise, a pleasant visit with Grandpa, as usual. I played with my daughter on the living room floor after supper while my wife corrected a pile of assignments she'd collected from her students at school that day.

When feeding time came, I silently watched my wife bear her breast to the eager lips of my hungry daughter, speaking to her in a gentle loving voice; my mind kept racing over Grandpa's story of Norma Crampton and the crying baby.

I think I understood, watching my wife sustain the life of our child, how Grandpa had explained to himself Mrs. Crampton's disappearance. Perhaps something in that house, perhaps even the soul of a dead, abandoned child, had sensed her need and had cried out to her. Or perhaps she had imagined the crying all along.

Whatever it was, Grandpa was right. She had found a purpose, a calling. And she'd answered it. I wondered what I could do for my Grandpa's loneliness. Particularly now that Norma was no longer in the nursing home. He'd mentioned her before, many times, and I knew, though he never said it in any specific words, that he had feelings for Norma Crampton. While their relationship would never have been anything more than friendship, at least they had that before she left.

Now, he had nothing again. Nobody close to confide in. Except for me once a week.

On the couch my daughter nursed serenely, her eyes returning my wife's absorbed attention. There was no way she would allow my guilt to compromise that bond. We had been through the discussion and argument many times, and it always came down to a decision between the generation that came before me or the one that came after me. My wife was right, of course. I had to focus on our daughter, on her future, and couldn't spend all my time on Grandpa's situation.

But that didn't make my guilt easier to live with.

It was the telephone call from the nursing home the next day that really did it for me.

Grandpa had disappeared some time in the middle of the night. They hadn't been able to find him anywhere.

I didn't even tell my wife. I couldn't have that conversation; not then, not feeling so much to blame for what had happened. I simply headed off to the nursing home to meet with the officials there and the police.

After some serious questioning, a bunch of obligatory paperwork and various other mundane details, I finally left the nursing home and walked to my car. I felt empty, and sat behind the wheel, staring vacantly. From the nursing home parking lot, I found myself looking at the big old house that had featured so strongly in Grandpa's story.

As I regarded the house, a thought hit me, and a small glimmer of hope. There was something about the things Grandpa had told me. About an old person getting lonely, longing for someone to look after. And the panicky way he made me promise not to tell anyone this story.

I found myself cutting through the hedges, crossing the lawn and heading up the walk to the front porch. Sure enough, the front door was boarded over—at least I had tried.

Halfway back to the car I quite unaccountably turned toward the house again, went back and started prying those boards off with my bare hands. Luckily, they were weathered. The nails pulled out with high pitched squeals; after a few minutes, I was able to enter the front door.

I stood in the dark and dusty entranceway and surveyed the room. All the furniture was there, covered in undisturbed dust. There was no sign of anyone having entered the house before me for a long, long time. I felt as if I were violating a tomb, and was about to turn and leave when I heard it: a soft creaking noise coming from the second floor.

I listened harder, unable to move any further. Then came the distinct sound of a woman's voice, cooing and lulling. Then footsteps overhead. The creaking stopped. The lulling, motherly voice continued, getting louder, and then another series of footsteps crossed the floor, stopping when a deeper voice, slightly lower in volume, floated an indistinct query. The female voice said something in response and the male voice chuckled softly.

Then both sets of footsteps resumed, moving this time in a leisurely but inexorable fashion towards the top of the stairs.

I stood in place, rooted in the fear of what I might see coming around the corner at the top of the stairway. Something that apparently didn't leave tracks in the dust.

Finally, I tore myself from the spot and bolted from the house. Without looking back, I got into my car and went home.

Sure, I'll admit to being too afraid to stay in that house to confirm my suspicion, but how much more proof did I need? Besides, was I really, or will I ever be prepared to accept what I might have seen at the top of the stairway?

Despite the impossibility of what I was thinking, it came down to one simple thing.

The gentle motherly and contented male voice I had heard upstairs were those of a happy couple—two old people who again had a purpose in life.

Shouldn't that be enough?

Spirits

Mark Leslie

Originally appeared as a stand-alone eBook in Spirits: A Haunting Love Story, *Stark Publishing, 2011.*

S itting here on the bus stop bench is startlingly comfortable, even though the sheets of misty rain have already cut through my jacket, plastering my shirt to my skin.

The cold dampness doesn't bother me.

Because my mind is otherwise occupied.

By thoughts of Sally.

I haven't thought about her in years; ever since I left Ottawa, actually. But now that I'm back, back here, especially, the vacant lot across from where I'm sitting — the lot where the old Phoenix *movie theatre used to stand — stares back at me and reminds me of her.*

Reminds me of that night.

* * *

"Do you believe in spirits?" Sally asked, the flashlight throwing long shadows up her face.

"You mean ghosts?" Rob admired how her features could still seem attractive even in such an eerie light.

"No," Sally said, her face disappearing as the flashlight clicked off. He heard the echoes of her movements in the large empty theatre. The complete darkness, coupled with the serious tone in her voice, was suddenly unsettling. "Not ghosts. Spirits."

"There's a difference?"

"Uhuh," Something touched his hand in the darkness. At first he flinched and tried to pull away. Then he realized it was Sally's hand.

He squeezed.

She squeezed back.

He let out a deep breath. For a moment he had been uneasy, but things were okay again. That's how their relationship seemed to work. That was why they were in this abandoned movie theatre after all.

Rob was making plans to go away to college and they had been talking about the consequences of his moving to a city four hours away while she stayed in Ottawa. They each got a bad feeling about being separated like that, and so they did what they usually did when they were having a minor crisis. They came to the place where they'd had their first date: *The Phoenix*.

What they had meant to each other that evening of their first date -- what their entire relationship meant -- came back to them whenever they went inside. As corny as it had seemed to their friends, it had become a ritual that worked for them.

Only now, the theatre was closed down and boarded up.

But they didn't let that stop them. It was exciting actually. One of the things Rob had always liked about Sally was her sense of excitement, of adventure: Her spirit.

And she was definitely showing it tonight.

Sneaking to the back of the abandoned building in the middle of the night; climbing the fire escape to the roof; prying the old service door open and slipping inside; scrambling through the darkness with the light of a single flashlight beam to guide them; finding their way into the theatre house; making out in the darkness. Yes, this was the gist of what Sally and Rob were all about.

"A ghost," Sally said, nestling herself onto Rob's lap. "Is a specter. It's supposed to represent the lost soul of someone who has died."

"Isn't that what a spirit is?"

"It can be. But a spirit can also be something more. For example, take my teddy."

"Pouffy Bear?" Rob giggled.

"Yeah. Now listen, I'm serious."

"Okay,"

"I've had him ever since I was a baby and I've always kept him close by. I talk to him. I sleep with him every night..."

"Hey, I'm jealous."

"Shush. And I shower him with love and affection."

"So?"

"Well, some people believe that because I've spent so much time with him, because I've projected so many emotions and feelings onto him, that Pouffy somehow absorbed it all and can feed it back to me."

"So you're saying that because you spent eighteen years loving him, that Pouffy, a stuffed animal, loves you?"

"Sort of." Sally shifted in his lap, turning to face him in the darkness. "When I'm sad or angry, I hold Pouffy Bear and he's able to make me feel better. I feel protected and safe whenever I hold him, because he provides me with a feeling of love and affection."

"An echo of the affection you've given him?"

"Yeah. But this doesn't just happen with objects," she said. "It can happen with a place. People who haven't died can still leave their spirit in a place. And they spend the rest of their lives searching for...something...because they have this empty feeling. They don't know what it is, though. They don't realize their spirit is still waiting for them at the place where they left it."

"Does this story have a point?"

"I'm getting to it. Here's the good part; the part that'll freak you out."

"I'm ready to be freaked."

She kissed him and then pulled away. "I've heard that this theatre has a spirit."

A chill ran down Rob's spine.

"It does?"

"Yeah. My Mom told me about something that happened here a long time ago. There was this lady who worked here at the popcorn stand. She was going out with the projectionist. Whenever they had a chance, they would, you know, get it on in the projection booth.

"Eventually, the woman got pregnant. And apparently, it ended up that she was also working here the evening she went into a premature labor. She went up to the projection booth to see her boyfriend and by the time she got to the top of the stairs, the baby started coming. She gave birth right here in the theatre."

"And the baby died and now haunts the theatre?" Rob asked, fidgeting in his seat.

"No. The baby lived. I think she gave it away for adoption, or something. But ever since that day, whenever they ran a film, some people could hear this strange sound — really faint — behind the soundtrack of the film. It was the sound of a baby crying."

"Where was it coming from?"

"They didn't know. 'Cause every time they stopped the film to listen, they couldn't hear it anymore. They could only hear it when a film was running. Nobody could figure it out."

Rob felt goose bumps rise along his arms.

"People said," she continued, "that what they were hearing was the spirit of the baby that had been born here. *The Phoenix Baby*, they called it."

"Oh, that's bull," Rob said. "It's one of those urban myths."

"My Mom said it was in the papers and everything."

"So what happened?"

"What do you mean?"

"Well, we've seen movies here and never heard the baby crying. When did the crying stop? And why?"

"I'm not sure. Maybe one day the baby returned -- all grown up -- to see a movie or something, and without knowing it, reclaimed the spirit left behind all those years ago."

"Aw, the whole story is made up."

"It is not. It's true." Sally leaned forward and began to imitate the cry of a baby.

Laughing, Rob ran his hands down her back and then feathered his fingers forward, across her ribs and up under her breasts.

"Oh. Tickles!" She squirmed, trying to get out of his lap.

He pulled her down, continuing to tickle her.

"Stop it stop it stop it," she laughed, ducking down under his arms.

Something hit the floor just beside them in the darkness.

"Now you've done it." Sally said, climbing from his lap. "That was the flashlight."

Rob cocked his head to hear the soft rumble of the flashlight as it rolled. It hit something, stopped for a second, and continued on. Then it hit something else and stopped for good.

"What now?" Rob asked.

"I guess now that we've lost our only source of light, the monsters will come out."

"Yeah, well that's only in movies. And this isn't a movie."

"But it is a movie theatre. The theatre with the spirit of *The Phoenix Baby*."

"What's gonna happen? Is a zombie baby going to attack us? Watch out, he's got a rattler!" He laughed. "But c'mon, I'm serious. How do we find our way out without the flashlight?"

Rob heard Sally shift in the seat beside him, felt the warmth of her bare arm as it brushed against his. For an obscure moment he had visions of the first time he'd brushed his lips against her bare skin and longed never to leave.

"We could guess our way back out," she said. "Or we could try to find the flashlight."

"What are the chances it rolled straight down to the very front?"

"Slim. We're about three quarters of the way up and it didn't sound like it rolled all the way down. Maybe only halfway."

She took his hand in the darkness.

He bent and kissed the back of her hand. "We'd better start looking, because when I make love to you here I want to be able to look into your gorgeous eyes."

"Keep talking,"

"I want to see the beautiful curve of your cheek, the silky magic of your hair cascading past your naked shoulders and over your..."

Sally sighed loudly and was up out of her seat. "Okay, let's find the flashlight."

"I'll tell you one thing, though," Rob said as they moved down the slope of the aisle to start their search. "I've never been bored on a date with you."

"Thanks,"

"I've been horny, excited, stimulated. Sometimes pissed off, lost, and trapped in the dark in an abandoned movie theatre. But never bored."

She pulled her hand away. "Jerk!"

"No, I mean it, Sally. As strange a situation as we're in right now, I'm glad I'm in it with you. I'm glad we came here again. Being with you, no matter what we're doing, makes me realize you're very special. I can't imagine being without you when I go away to school. Sally, I lo– "

A loud crash echoed through the darkness.

"What was that?" Sally whispered.

Rob whipped his head around. "Where did it come from?"

"I couldn't tell with the echo. But it sounded like something metal falling."

"Did it fall over on its own, or did someone knock it over?"

"Okay, time to find the flashlight."

Holding hands, they descended a number of rows and felt around in the dark for the flashlight. They worked methodically and quietly.

When they'd checked three aisles, Sally spoke up. "Maybe it was nothing, you know. Maybe a small animal knocked something over. Rats or mice."

His hand bumped against something. "Wait a second."

"What? Did you find it?"

He wrapped his hand around a cylindrical object. The flashlight. He picked it up and stood.

"Did you find it?" she asked again, grabbing his arm with both her hands.

"Yeah," he said and put his free arm around her.

She hugged him back, and then pulled away.

"So?"

Rob ran his hand along the plastic case of the flashlight.

"Well," she said. "Turn it on."

"I'm afraid to. What if I turn it on and it doesn't work? What if it broke when it hit the seats?"

She grabbed it from him. "Don't say things like that. Jeez. Let's just turn it on and get out of here."

"Well?" Rob said. He waited a moment. It was still pitch-black. "Well, turn it on."

Her voice was solemn. "I just did."

The distinct sound of a door slamming shut echoed through the theatre.

"That wasn't a rat or mouse," Rob whispered. "Vermin don't use doors. Maybe the sound was the owner or something. Or maybe...oh boy."

"What?"

"It could be the police. Maybe someone saw us sneaking around on the roof and called the cops on us."

"But we didn't do anything. We aren't vandals."

"It's still 'breaking-and-entering' even if we didn't break anything."

They stood in silence for a moment.

Sally nudged him. "There's no light anywhere. If the owner or the police were inside, wouldn't they at least have a flashlight?"

"You're right."

"So maybe that door closing was the sound of them leaving." She took his hand. "And if so, we'd better split before they come back in."

They moved up the aisle, shuffling slowly to the top of the theatre house.

"There are three stairwells here." Rob said.

"Yeah. We came down the middle one. That leads to the upper floor, doesn't it?"

"I think so."

Still holding hands, they went up the stairs. At the top, Rob felt along the wall. They inched their way forward until his hand came upon a doorknob. He turned it and pushed. The heavy door opened.

"Is this it?"

"Not sure," He paused and guided her free hand to hold the door once he passed through so it wouldn't slam in her face. Then he walked forward. After a few more steps, the door sprang back and shut loudly behind them.

They both jumped. "Sorry," Sally muttered.

They giggled and moved forward until Rob kicked something small. It clattered along the cement floor, a hollow tinny sound.

"Whoops,"

He walked around it and his outstretched hand hit a wall of brick. He felt sideways along the coarse brick until his hand slipped off into open space then hit something just as solid but very smooth. Glass.

"What the...?"

"We came the wrong way, didn't we?"

"I think so." He turned and wrapped both his arms around her. She hugged him back. Something in one of her hands dug into his back as she held him.

"What's that in your hand?"

"Oh. It's the, ah, flashlight."

"But it's broken. You may as well pitch it. It's no good to us now."

There was a long pause before Sally spoke. "Rob,"

"Yeah?"

"I don't want to let go of it." Her trembling voice broke on the last word.

Rob held her tightly as she shook with silent tears.

Suddenly, a small flash of light filled the room to the sound of something hitting the floor beside them.

They both gasped.

"It's working," Sally said. "When I dropped it, it came on for a second."

Rob released her and knelt in, feeling along the floor. He found it and shook it. The light flashed on briefly yet again.

"What did you do?"

"I joggled it a bit. Maybe when we first dropped it the impact misaligned the batteries or something."

"Do it again."

The light came on. This time it stayed on. There was enough light for Rob to see her face again, and the look of concern in her eyes was unsettling. He'd never seen such a pained look before and almost wished the light would go out again so he wouldn't have to see it.

"So where exactly are we?" He turned and aimed the beam at the wall. Set into the brick was a thin rectangular window.

"We're in the projection room," Sally muttered. Rob twisted to face her again and saw her looking down at an empty film canister. Then he passed the beam along the floor to a small narrow mattress perched on a makeshift cot up against the far wall. On top of this cot were a couple of worn and battered blankets.

"Someone lives here," Sally said.

"Okay, that's our cue to leave." He pulled on her arm and started to move toward the door, but stopped almost immediately.

Blocking the doorway stood a tall gangly man.

*   *   *

Being inside the cafe across the street from the empty theatre lot warms my damp, wrinkled skin, just as the coffee I cradle before me warms my insides.

But a chill still runs deep inside that neither the warm room nor the coffee can curb.

The exact moment of staring him directly in the face has returned to me in countless nightmares. I'd wake up screaming, covered in a cold sweat, with the image of those deeply shadowed eye sockets within which I could never make out the eyes. I always knew he was staring at me, though, staring right through me. But for the life of me, each time I dreamt of that pale thin face and those hauntingly sunken eyes, I could never remember where he was from.

It comes back to me now, though.

It all comes back to me how my immediate reaction was to flash the light in his face and then stab the flashlight into his stomach. The gangly man doubled over easily and I shoved him out of the doorway. As he staggered back against the wall, I kicked him in the ribs, brought the flashlight down on his skull and pounded both of my elbows onto his back. As he crumpled to the floor, I hauled Sally out the doorway and past him.

Both of us screaming, we somehow picked the right stairway and ran for the exit.

The rest of that night is still a blur.

But what happened between us next, that's all becoming startlingly clear.

* * *

"Why haven't you called?"

"I've been busy. Look, Rob, I can't talk now."

"Sally, wait..."

The dial tone was his only answer. For the past three weeks, that had been the only type of answer she'd given him. A closed door, a dial tone -- it was all the same. He wondered if it was because of his violent reaction to the stranger and the fact both Sally and Rob were convinced that Rob's attack had seriously injured or killed him. He'd never behaved that way before and had only done so that night out of self-defense and fear. After all, they had no idea what the stranger had intended to do to them.

And Rob did make an anonymous call to 911 telling them about an injured man in the abandoned theatre. But there was nothing about a mysterious death or injury that night in any of the local media.

And he couldn't get her to admit that was why she was avoiding him because she wouldn't even speak to him for more than the words it took to say goodbye.

He stared at the phone receiver a while longer and then slammed it down.

Enough was enough. He'd have to march over to her place and confront her. He felt bad enough about his attack on the stranger. He needed Sally's reassurance that he'd done it to protect them. He just couldn't go on like this.

When he arrived at her parents' home, he knocked and waited.

No answer.

He knocked again. Harder.

Still no answer.

Her father's car was not in the driveway, and given that it was Sunday it meant they were probably visiting Sally's Grandmother at the nursing home. But Sally never went with them. She couldn't handle seeing her Grandmother kept like an animal in a zoo, treated like she was too dumb and frail to handle being outside of that protective cage. Stored away only to be seen by the outside world during pre-allotted visiting time slots.

The more he thought of it the more he was sure he needed to explain to her his violent reaction that night.

Rob knocked again, waited, then tried the door.

It was unlocked. He pushed it open.

"Hello?"

No answer.

He walked inside. The house was quiet and very much like a museum with its antique furniture, artwork and sculptures all lit with their own small sets of lights. He'd never felt very comfortable in either the living room or dining room and could never imagine having grown up in such a house. There were so many fragile looking things to break.

He looked across at the stairs which led up to Sally's room, the only cozy room in the house. Perhaps she had headphones on and couldn't hear him knocking. It had happened before.

He headed up the stairs and was about to call out once more when a strange thought struck him.

What if she's not alone? After all, the best time Sally and Rob could sneak in some frisky playtime was on Sundays when her parents were out of the house for several hours. What if the reason she'd been avoiding him was because there was some other guy?

He froze. He couldn't move, couldn't decide what he should do. Should he just accept that she was with someone else and leave? No. After all, he had no proof. It would be stupid to leave with that assumption. But it would also be stupid to walk in on Sally and some other guy rolling naked beneath the sheets. The thought turned his stomach.

No, he had to give her the benefit of the doubt.

And, regardless, if she didn't want him in her life, she'd have to tell him to his face.

Fixing his determination, he headed up the stairs. Her bedroom door was closed. He paused again, listening. If she was with someone, it would be fair to make some noise to let them know that they weren't alone.

He coughed.

Waited.

Then reached for the doorknob.

Something sharp dug into the back of his right ankle, and he spun around sending a fist into empty air. His foot kicked out and he felt a small weight clinging to it. His kick, combined with the unstopped punch, threw him off balance and he fell against Sally's door. Reaching out for balance, he knocked over a skinny table with a vase. The vase broke as it hit the floor. The tiny furry thing attached to Rob's ankle released its hold and bolted down the stairs, letting out a high-pitched battle cry.

Rob grabbed his ankle. "Cootie, you little bastard!"

He shook his head while examining the tiny bite marks Cootie, Sally's cat had left on his ankle.

To Sally, the cat was loving and tender, existing only to rub against her and seek affection. But whenever Sally left the room, the cat had never once failed to assert hatred towards Rob. It glared at him, hissed at him, swiped at him, attacked his feet. Almost as if it were jealous of Sally's affection for Rob.

Discovering that his ankle wasn't bleeding, he got to his feet and stood in front of the bedroom door. Whatever had been going on in there, there had been plenty of warning to become presentable.

He knocked then opened the door. But there was nobody inside.

Now he felt like he was trespassing. It seemed okay to enter the house when he thought someone was home and they just couldn't hear him knocking. But now it suddenly felt wrong.

He walked over to her desk to find a piece of paper and a pencil. He'd leave a note explaining why he'd come, how he'd thought she was here and how the vase in the hall had gotten broken.

When he got to the desk, he paused.

Something seemed different about her room.

Sally's room had always been plastered with posters, clippings, photos and mementos from her life and they served to promote the variety of who she was. There were photos of the people in her life, postcards from family and friends around the world, ticket stubs from concerts she'd been to, even bus transfers from "important" bus rides she'd taken. And it had always fascinated Rob that a good way to decipher how Sally felt at any given time was to see what new items she had strewn about her desk, tacked to the bulletin board and taped to the edges of her dresser mirror.

Sally always had something pinned, taped or hanging in her room. But it was always varied — if you could call it anything, you'd have to call it eclectic.

But now –– only three weeks since he'd last been here –– that was what was different.

As Rob scanned the contents of the desk, the items stuck to her bulletin board and the photos taped to her mirror, he found one thing in common. They all had something to do with *The Phoenix*.

There were photos of both the outside and inside of the theatre plastered all over her mirror. There was a floor plan of the entire building with specific sections marked off in red pen.

He noted some of the headlines on photocopied newspaper articles from the early fifties.

CRY OF THE PHOENIX BABY!

PHOENIX BABY HAUNTS PATRONS, MYSTIFIES POLICE

Quickly scanning through the articles, Rob noted they verified the story Sally had told him that night in the theatre. He flipped through the articles until he found another large headline dated almost two decades later.

THE CRYING AT THE PHOENIX STOPS

The article explained that for no apparent reason, the crying simply ceased. There was a photo of a man standing near the projectors. The caption read: "Greg Bartholomew, projectionist at *The Phoenix*, ponders the mystery of *The Phoenix Baby*. 'I've never heard it myself, since I just started working here, but I can't believe that all those people were just hearing things. Something strange had to have been going on.'"

Rob stared at the photo again.

There was something familiar about the man, something he couldn't quite place.

Then it hit him.

Bartholomew was tall, very thin, almost gangly. In the photo his eyes were shadowed by a protruding brow.

It couldn't be.

Rob looked over at the photos bordering the edge of Sally's mirror. They were all shots of Greg Bartholomew, only he looked more gangly, his eyes more sunken than the photo from the 70's. He looked more like he did when they saw him a few weeks ago in the doorway of the projection room. One was a profile of him walking down the street after dark. Another was him standing in a back alley, digging in a garbage can for something. The third, taken almost straight on, was him leaning against a building, hand out, head down –- begging. And all of the photos had that slightly blurry quality you see on "candid" tabloid shots. They were all taken at weird angles, as if from behind a parked car, around the corner of a building, or from a moving vehicle.

Sally was obsessed with this man. What could she possibly be up to?

"What are *you* doing here?" The words dug into him the same way Cootie's teeth had.

Rob spun and his jaw dropped open. He knew it was Sally, but she never looked like this, never looked so worn and unconcerned about her appearance, never looked so –- disheveled. It was as if she'd given up focusing on anything but *The Phoenix* and Greg Bartholomew.

Like a monk devoting his life to God, Sally seemed to have forsaken all other things.

"Well?"

"Sally? What are you doing? These articles? These pictures?"

"That's my business."

"Why haven't you talked to me? Why haven't you told me about any of this? God, I've been worried sick that I might have killed a man, and you couldn't tell me you have proof he's okay?"

"I *told* you I don't want to see you or talk to you. I told you to leave me alone."

"Sally, please talk to me. I didn't mean to hurt him. It was self de..."

"Get out, Rob. I'm busy."

"Busy with what? With stalking this man? What are you doing? He's a homeless bum. He's crazy."

"He's not crazy."

"How do you know?"

"He's the *Phoenix Baby*."

"What?"

"He's the Phoenix Baby. He left his spirit there when he was born. When he returned, as an adult, to work as the projectionist, the crying stopped. Don't you get it, Rob? Don't you understand? His only destiny was to return to the theatre and reclaim his spirit. But now he's tied to that spot, because his spirit is tying him there. He can't leave without leaving his spirit behind. He needs my help."

"He needs to be locked away. He's nuts. He could hurt you, Sally. Don't go near him anymore. Stay away from him."

"He won't hurt me." she said, and a strange look entered her eyes.

"Sally. You're not...you don't mean? You don't love him do you?"

Her face paled at those words but she said nothing.

"You don't know what you're getting into. He could seriously hurt you."

"The same way you hurt him? If I have anyone to fear right now, it's you."

"You never let me explain. He's clouding your judgment. Please, stay away from him and give me a chance to explain."

"Don't tell me what to do."

"Please, Sally, you need help."

"I *need* you to leave me alone."

"Sally," Rob stepped toward her. She flinched, as if she thought he would strike her. And that more than any of her words, let him know that he'd lost her. He hung his head down and stepped back.

"Rob, I have to do this. I must do this. I can't explain but I need you to leave."

He turned and looked at Pouffy sitting on her bed and taking in the entire scene. *Take care of her*, he thought to the bear. Fighting back tears, he walked past her, out the room, out of her life, and never spoke with her since.

*   *   *

Losing her love, losing her trust, that was the hardest blow I'd ever faced. It hurt me so deeply. It still hurts. The waitress who just refilled my coffee can see my tears, but I don't care. The emotions come back with an incredible intensity as I sit here and remember in a silent reunion with the painful memories.

Maybe that was why I blocked most of it out, chose not to remember. Maybe that was why I was never able to have a successful relationship with anyone since then. Maybe that was why my marriage failed after only six months. Perhaps I was afraid the best thing for any woman that I'd grown to care about was to leave her alone. Irrational, I know. But often your first important relationship affects the rest in the subtlest and most powerful ways.

But now that I remember, now that I recall the scene in Sally's bedroom, the choice I made to leave her alone, I wonder if I really did the right thing. Should I have tried to help her? Should I have persisted? Whatever happened to her after that? And was it my fault?

I kept tabs on her, very secretly, of course, the way the rejected party often does at the end of a relationship. I remember listening in when a group of friends were talking about her and hearing stories that one day she'd simply disappeared, ran off somewhere, leaving a note to her parents to say goodbye. And I remember thinking it had been my fault.

Why hadn't I helped her?

Then again, I sometimes think perhaps she united with Greg Bartholomew. Maybe they were destined to be together. Maybe she nursed him back into society with her gentle and caring ways. And if that's what made her happy then I guess it was for the best.

But that still doesn't make it hurt any less.

I grasp my coffee cup and gaze out into the rain. It's still misty, but easier to see through. As I stare at the empty lot where the theatre used to be, I swear I can hear something.

Crying.

Even through the window, through the rain, across the street and over the sound of traffic, I can hear a soft crying.

My eyes pierce the darkness of the lot, scan every corner, until I see, propped up against the north wall, a pile of garbage from the furniture shop next door. Amidst the cardboard boxes and garbage bags, there's a thin dark human-shaped form.

That small, thin shape, huddled to fight the rain, and the crying piercing my ears.

Him.

The building went down years ago, but he never left.

He couldn't.

His spirit tied him there.

I pull a bill from my wallet and leave it on the table. Then I walk out of the cafe, instantly re-soaked, chilled.

The crying is louder.

Now I'm certain I'll finally get my answer.

I cross the street, shivering and wet, but not caring. I move past the bus stop, across the sidewalk and approach the pile of garbage. The crying becomes an intense buzzing in my ears, a mantra that pulls me forward.

The lone figure huddled there without protection from the elements seems to mock me, my life, all that I've taken for granted. Guilt courses through me again for remembering how

I'd struck him that night years ago out of fear. And fear over what? A helpless, undernourished man living hand to mouth ever since the theatre closed down? A man whose only home now is the discarded refuse of a retail outlet on a barren lot? I think I finally understand Sally's unselfish sense of compassion and duty.

I take my jean jacket off and lay it on the still body.

I stand, confused, with the sound of crying ringing in my ears and a feeling of emptiness.

For a second, I wonder if he's dead.

But there is movement again. The body shifts, the head slowly turns up, the eyes meet mine.

Then I realize.

It's her.

My eyes fill with tears as Sally looks up at me.

"I knew you'd eventually return, my love," she says weakly and smiles. In her eyes I can see the response to all of my questions and my heart aches at the obvious answer and all the lost years.

I drop to the ground and hold her.

The crying stops.

SCOTT OVERTON

No Walls

Scott Overton

Originally appeared in Neo-opsis *magazine, Issue #18, Dark Opus Press, October 2011.*

I almost died the first time I learned that I could walk through walls.

At least you no longer laugh at the concept. That's progress. But then you know better. My guards do not, so they laugh. Of course they laugh. They've never seen me do it. If I could do it here I would have escaped long before now — that much is obvious to anyone.

You know better because you've seen it, used it. Used me.

I'm not bitter anymore. Without you and your Institute I'd never have had a scientific explanation for what happens to me. I might still believe that I'd permanently slipped a cog and was living in some schizophrenic hallucination. (I never tried to spend the money from that bank, you know. Part of me couldn't believe it was real.)

I was desperate for an explanation—you can't know what it's like. At least Pearson's theories about interpenetrating universes offered one possible means of rationalizing the irrational. A straw I could grasp. Your Dr. Storck simply said the model fit the observable facts in my case. But I know he was glad he didn't have to try to convince the rest of the scientific community. Give up on their precious Einstein? I don't expect to live to see it. But then I don't expect to live to see tomorrow.

And that first time it happened I didn't know anything about the parallel universe theories. I just knew that I turned the wrong direction in a thirteenth floor office suite and instead of slamming into a triple-paned window I found myself in the open air with one foot on a ten-inch ledge and the other on...nothing. Nothing of our material universe, anyway. Maybe in that other place it was the protruding end of a two-by-four because that version of the building was still under construction. I don't know. In the bright sunlight I couldn't see it. I couldn't see anything but thirteen floors' worth of empty space between me and the hard pavement. If I'd stopped for even a moment, I would have lost my balance or fainted. Instead, my automatic reaction was to step backward, without thinking of what my right foot could be pushing against. And then I was back inside the room. Behind the glass. The whole thing could not have taken more than a few seconds.

I knew I must have been hallucinating. The mind can't accept something like that and just reject the construct of reality, built up over a lifetime.

It happened again a couple of weeks later. I've told you about that one. I desperately wanted to read my boss's analysis of the report I'd just given him. My career hung on it. Some of the report was going to make him look bad, and I'd need to defend myself when we brought it to the Board. I even made an excuse to stay late that night, hoping against hope that he'd leave his office door unlocked. He didn't. But as I leaned on the polished wood, trying to plan my next step, suddenly I was inside the office, and the papers were lying on his desk.

I couldn't explain it—didn't even try. I had what I wanted and that was all that mattered at the time. It was later, calming my nerves at a bar down the street that the first incident came back to me, and I began to try to make the pieces fit.

I felt like a God that night. I wasn't rational, I know that. A heady mix of hubris and eight ounces of Scotch led me to a way to test my theory at the YMCA next door. The attendant was busy watching TV as I made my way to the swimming pool area. The men's shower was unoccupied, as I'd hoped, but I could hear water running in the women's shower next door. On the other side of one thin wall. I had no control over my ability yet. I thought it somehow responded to desire, and I had plenty right then. Maybe too much—nothing happened. But as I began to wonder why, I sensed the change. A moment out of time. An orphan instant. My heart sometimes skips a beat—it was like that.

I slid through the wall and steam surrounded me. Four naked women were soaping their slick bodies and pivoting slowly in the hot spray. Two of them were white with athletic builds, smooth skin and small breasts. The third woman was black and heavier but with ostentatious curves. I've only reconstructed the scene from memory (and more often lately, in this god-forsaken place) because the reality lasted only seconds. The fourth woman began to scream.

Of course she saw me. Thanks to the alcohol it never occurred to me that incorporeal didn't mean invisible. And in my shock the walls stayed completely impenetrable, too. I was just damned lucky that the adjoining pool area had an outside door, and no pursuers were fast enough to follow my wet footprints.

Now you're laughing.

*   *   *

The guards have arrived. Two of them. The first few days they mainly ignored me, except to turn the lights on for different intervals at all hours. To mess up my time sense, mess with my mind, I know. I've read my share of spy novels. They're trying to 'soften me up'. For the same reason, I never know when my next meal's coming either. At first, I tried not to eat anything—afraid of drugs, or something disgusting they might have put in it—but you can't keep that up.

One of them comes into the room. I'm sitting on the floor, so he just stands over me, staring me down, not speaking. Five minutes. Maybe ten. Then he unzips his pants and pulls out his manhood. I think he's going to piss on me.

At the last moment he diverts the stream and it hits the floor beside me. I can still feel the warm spray, and turn my head in shame.

When he's finished, he bends down near my ear and whispers, "Say your prayers. Soon you will die." They are gone before I can bring myself to look up.

*   *   *

I never read any physics until this happened to me, and afterward I could still only stomach the popular treatments: Hawking and Feynman digested in small pieces while riding the commuter train to work. They couldn't provide the answers I needed, though. I thought about Everett's ideas of duplicate universes being created every time a moving particle has to make up its mind which way to go. Does anybody really buy that? Unthinkably complicated! And anyway, it didn't explain how my body could suddenly be able to ignore solid matter. At the Institute, the scenario Dr. Storck painted for me was elegant in its simplicity, and as plausible as I was likely to find. Even high school dropouts know that atomic structure is mostly empty space, so the idea of other universes of matter coexisting in the same space as ours, but at an incompatible frequency of energy (or wavelength—whichever is the case doesn't make any difference to me) didn't seem impossible. It was either that or believe that I was already a ghost without realizing it, like the guy in "The Sixth Sense". That thought crossed my mind a lot in the early days. It didn't appeal to me at all.

Besides, Storck's explanation fit what I experienced. He said the other universes 'interpenetrating' ours were like the frequencies of the radio band, but our bodies were set to 'tune in' only one frequency and ignore all others. The atoms of my body had somehow forgotten that lesson. Sometimes they could tune out the home frequency, and no longer recognize a solid wall or other object as being a barrier. Picture conga lines crossing at a party: our atoms mutually agreed to allow each other passage through the gaps between.

It feels like that. It feels like I'm mentally 'tuning' across a range of options, until I hit on one that works. And I'm convinced that it involves more than just one overlapping Earth. I have no idea how many. As I'm tuning out the frequency of our universe I must be tuning in the frequency of another. That's obvious, isn't it? Otherwise I'd drift out of position, or sink into the floor, but I don't. I'm still walking on something that's recognized as solid by the atoms of my feet. The only reason I can go through walls is that I tune in a world *where those walls don't exist*. Where the building has a slightly different layout, or doors that are often left open. Or where there is no building at all.

You didn't know that, did you? I don't think Storck did, either. I figured it out for myself.

My captors don't know it. They just got lucky.

After the fiasco at the 'Y', I was scared to try my ability anywhere but around my own home. The house was only five years old, so maybe that's why it was easy to tune in an otherworld version of it with no walls. A few times I even miscalculated and ran into two-by-fours of the building frame, but I soon learned to predict where they were and avoid them. Plumbing hurt more.

Yes, that was a joke, but also true. Think of the pitfalls of an ability like mine. At a certain stage buildings don't have walls, but before that they don't have floors either. I learned to be very cautious.

I never told my wife or daughter. My wife and I were always on the verge of divorce anyway (did you feed her some kind of story about my disappearance, or does she think I'm dead?) And my daughter? Well once I had a beautiful little girl. Then one day I woke up to find there was a stranger living in my house: a stranger with dyed black hair, Alice Cooper makeup, and pieces of metal hanging from every body part that wasn't already stained by ink. She once caught me coming out of her room. Somehow the fact that the door had never moved didn't register on her brain. What registered was that I'd invaded her privacy, and the screaming exchange that followed was the last conversation we ever had, if you can call it that.

You know what's funny? I think my bizarre behavior those last few days at home actually brought mother and daughter closer together. They'd always been like oil and water before, but despising me gave them something to share. I'm a man who can walk through walls. But only the physical kind.

*   *   *

The guards are back. This time I think they mean business. I don't know how many days it's been. I'm sure they're only leaving the lights off for two hours at a stretch—no more than that. I'm in a daze most of the time. The horrible food leaves me feeling sick, too.

There are shackles anchored in the wall. Two sets: high and low—I'm sitting right between the low ones. My captors have never used them on me, until now. I feel like vomiting as the metal bands lock around my wrists.

The guard that almost pissed on me bends over me and smiles. The other has stepped out of the cell.

"Why did they send you?" the first guard asks. The second one returns with something in his hand. It looks like a piece of shielded electrical cable.

Oh, God, no.

"Why did they send you?"

What can I answer? Do I try to pretend I'm innocent? Do I say I'm a spy?

Do I tell them I was sent because I can walk through walls?

I try to clear my throat, but I'm too late. The cable slices through the air.

Oh Christ! Oh Christ Jesus! I never knew anything could hurt like that! My battered feet instantly go into spasms.

"I'm not anybody!" I scream. "I'm not a spy! I'm a civilian. A civilian for Christ's..."

A whip crack.

My back arches off the dirt. I've bit my tongue—I can taste the blood.

"I can't...I don't know what to say! *What do you want me to say?*" Red spittle sprays my chest.

The air hisses in protest.

My head snaps against the rock-hard wall, and my eyes dim, flooded with tears.

The voice says, "Why did they send you?"

"*I can walk through walls! I can walk through walls!*" I babble.

There is the sound of their laughter. And then the whip scrapes across the floor, coiling to strike again.

*   *   *

Think about this: What would the average person do with a 'gift' like mine? Is it good for anything but larceny?

After a while I tried breaking into other homes on the street, just to see if I could do it. I was still a chickenshit— I wouldn't risk it unless I was certain no-one was home. Even then all I did was look around. I rifled through drawers and found valuables in absurdly obvious hiding places—one time even a stack of hundred-dollar bills in a fake stereo speaker. But I couldn't take them. Couldn't steal them. Not just because it felt wrong, but because it felt...petty. I had an ability that no-one else in the world could claim. Was I going to use it to become one of the bottom-feeding scavengers I despised so much? A contemptible sneak thief? The truth is, my only real thrill was when I mistakenly thought my lawyer neighbor's wife had gone out, and instead found her entertaining a young delivery man with his special package in her living room. I watched for about twenty minutes, then quietly made my way to the front door, slammed it, and yelled, "Jessica, I came home early."

I hid in the bushes long enough to see the man run naked from the back deck, then scrambled away myself.

Strange, how I could reject the vocation of burglar but embrace the role of voyeur. Freud might have been able to explain it. I didn't bother.

It wasn't that I couldn't physically steal things, either. Objects touching me travel with me. One of those small mercies. You've read or seen some version of the "Invisible Man" story—we all have. The poor bugger always had to leave a trail of clothes behind! A modern DNA lab would have a field day with that. At least I didn't have to put up with the inconvenience of nudity. Maybe that's why I finally decided I could get away with robbing a bank.

Anyone can tell you that a man who wouldn't dream of snatching an old lady's purse doesn't have the same scruples when it comes to knocking over a bank. They deserve it. I told myself if I could make one big score I could immediately retire from both bank robbery and my usual form of thievery: brokering stock.

The thing about robbing a bank vault is, you have to defeat all of the security systems, get into the locked vault, and then get away clean. If you can't disable the security cameras you have to make sure you can't be identified. And if you can't be absolutely certain you won't trigger an alarm of some kind, you have to be able to beat it before the security guards or cops show up.

I picked a bank that was built a couple of years ago. It was planted on an outcrop of rock, so they weren't worried about tunnels, and it stood on its own about a hundred feet from the other buildings in the strip mall, and seventy or eighty feet from a Greek restaurant and a row of connected townhouses that shared the same back alley. Driving by at night I never saw any signs of life: no guards and thankfully no dogs. So that left the video cameras I could spot and a few hidden ones, plus I assumed an array of various motion detectors, probably sensitive to body heat too. I couldn't avoid any of those things and I didn't have a clue about hacking them by computer, or even hacking away at a box of wires somewhere. I only had one advantage. But it was one they couldn't have foreseen.

I walked six blocks to the bank that night, after parking on a residential street with lots of other cars. It was a little after midnight, so the streets still had some traffic. The alley behind the building included a couple of large garbage bins for the Greek restaurant. I hid behind one of those for a while, working up my nerve and pulling the balaclava over my face, then walked up to the wall of the bank and through it without stopping. I'd been practicing.

No doubt I triggered the alarms right away, but I went straight into the vault, reached into the special cabinets for the cash, filled a black canvas bag with it, and exited the same way I'd come in, clutching the bag tightly to my chest. Then I went around the corner of the first townhouse, out of sight of the bank cameras, and ghosted my way through walls and hallways to the far end of the row a block away. I was dressed in nondescript dark work clothes, padded with newspaper to make me look fifty pounds heavier for the sake of the video, so at the last house I disposed of the newspaper and put the money in its place around my body. The balaclava too. By then a couple of cop cars had gone by. I wasn't too worried. I'm sure by the time they figured out that nobody was going to come out of the bank vault, and looked at the security videos, I was safely in my bed. Thanks to her usual four vodkas, my wife never knew I'd left the house.

Do you remember Storck's assistant's name? It's Amber. You probably only remember her 36-inch C-cups. I do too, don't get me wrong. But she genuinely wanted to help me, so I think of her often. You only asked, "What can you do? How do you do it?" Amber thought to ask, "How do you *feel* about what's happened to you?"

When drunk, I felt like a god. When sober, like a freak. I was rarely sober. I drank because it was better than crying.

The worst part was the nightmares: I dreamed that the change grew steadily worse until one day I simply dissolved into a shadow and never came back.

Amber was in the room one time when I woke up with a scream. She told me the 'overlapping' worlds theory might explain some of our dreams. Maybe a lot of psychic phenomena, too. It might be that mediums tap into the parallel worlds with their minds, believing them to be 'higher planes of reality' that we go to when we die.

I can't testify to any of that. Not yet. But sometimes I can see the other places, in dim light, and I suppose people there might also be able to see me. So maybe I am a ghost after all.

*   *   *

The guards left me alone for...it feels like several days, though I still can't stand for long on my mangled feet. Now they've come back. This time the whip man carries two cables: electrical cables, stretching from somewhere beyond the door. There's a motor sound: a generator?

Live electrical cables.

The talker shows his bad teeth, but doesn't waste any time.

"Why did they send you?" he hisses.

I try to shake my head, speechless with horror. The second man doesn't even wait for an answer...touches the bare wires to my torso.

I scream until my lungs are empty.

They're saying something, but I can't make it out. It doesn't matter. I can't work my mouth to talk. The wires touch my abdomen.

I'm hearing noises. Animal noises. They couldn't be from a human being. Couldn't be from me.

The guard touches the wires to my genitals.

When the blackness fades and I become aware again, the first guard is gone. The second sees that I'm awake and raises his arm. The electrical wires are gone. The flog of shielded cable comes slashing down across my ribs.

I want to die. *Please just let me die.* My life hasn't been worth living anyway.

I didn't even feel the third blow. Heard the crack against the floor but felt nothing.

Wait! I really did feel nothing. No contact at all.

I force my eyes open to watch. The cable slices toward my body...*and through it!* It strikes the floor with a snap.

The guard hasn't seen. He's not really paying attention—so inured to brutalizing his fellow man that he's bored by it. I have enough sense to mimic my earlier cries of pain, but he'll have to notice something soon. Notice that his victim's skin hasn't peeled like it should. That there's no blood.

They'll kill me. Once they understand what I am, they'll have to. They'll *want* to. It's what I thought I wanted too, only seconds ago. But now?

God, it's such a blessed relief to escape the agony.

But there might be a way to stay alive. And to do that there is a price to pay.

A whimper escapes from my throat as my body understands what's coming next. I will myself to become solid, and scream as the flail comes lashing down.

*   *   *

The superhero comics write about Kryptonite, but they never mention the truly fatal flaw of the powerful: *terminal cockiness*. I was more than human, therefore I was untouchable. I knew it was true because the alcohol told me so.

So I concocted the scheme to break into your headquarters.

Of course, my newspaper padding didn't fool your mass analyzers. My mask was no protection from your thermal imaging software. And it was child's play to track my car by satellite. Then I was a mouse in a trap.

You had both the carrot and the stick: I could be a patriot or go to jail. And the first few times I actually felt like a hero when you had me ransack the homes of those congressmen and senators in the interest of 'safeguarding democracy'. Then I read a few of those stolen files, and realized I was being played for a sucker.

You were even ready for that. I'd thought only gangsters would threaten a man's family.

That was a line you shouldn't have crossed. Remember that. You're going to regret it.

But for now the only thing that's burning your ass is knowing that you've squandered a priceless resource, a one-of-a-kind commodity. *Me.*

We both know it was madness to send me to the Middle East. The *jihadists* can sniff out an outsider. Or maybe you thought that wouldn't matter, because I had a talent for escape that Houdini would have given his right arm for?

Then it was just bad luck that you sent me against a terror cell whose headquarters was in a mountain cave.

Did you know that caves and mountains exist unchanged for thousands of years in this world...and the next? And in every world I've tried.

I've had no way to escape, and no answers the guards will accept as truth, to bargain my way to freedom. So there's not much doubt they'll carry out their threat to execute me tonight.

Will you lose sleep over that? Probably not. So how about this:

I convinced you that electronic equipment didn't function through the transition to and from the other universes. That was a lie. A miniature camera I bought worked perfectly. I just wanted a record of my 'assignments' to use as an insurance policy. Now I see it as a cleansing flame to sterilize a plague.

For the first time in a long time I want to live, if only long enough to make one phone call.

One call, and a series of packages will find their way to several powerful (and uncompromised) congressmen. The top echelon of *Mossad*, and even the wealthy backers of my captors will all find the contents very enlightening. Your administration's time will be at an end, and a rift might even begin to heal. A carefully constructed *wall* might begin to crumble.

You can call me naïve. We'll see. If I fail, it means I don't escape a trap and you do. Either way, I have a feeling you'll get this message.

Don't even think about a reprisal against my family. It's far too late for that.

I can hear scraping noises at the door. The guards have come for me.

I've never tested it, but I have hopes that my transitional body can be convinced to deny the solidity of bullets and swords as well as walls and whips. The trick will be to maintain that state long enough to shake off any pursuit. The odds are against it, but I've had some time to practice. Maybe I'll even see Amber again.

If it doesn't work, well, I'm not all that afraid of Death anymore.

I've already been there.

Once Upon a Midnight

Scott Overton

Originally appeared in In Poe's Shadow, *edited by A.W. Gifford and Jennifer L. Gifford, Oct 2011*

In the end, the fate of humanity rested in the hands of a woman scorned.

Lennie Allen wouldn't have characterized herself in that way. But she'd already triggered one warning from the computer's security subroutine by being distracted. The next time she'd be locked out for twenty-four hours. The Director would not be amused.

Normally she welcomed the security protocols; the retina scan, voice recognition, code-words, and finger-print-scanning mouse were all a part of life in one of the nation's highest-echelon research facilities, and they helped her sleep at night. God knew, the stuff they handled could be used with catastrophic effect by the wrong people. It was the *keystroke dynamics* keyboard that turned out to be a pain in the ass. If its biometrics system ever suspected that she was acting under duress it would offer only two warnings and then go into complete lockdown. Mendelssohn swore he'd been locked out once as a result of chugging one too many Starbucks.

Lennie was finding it hard to care about invented global cataclysm when her own world was falling apart.

She loved working in WCSD — the development and analysis of *worst-case scenarios* made good use of her vivid imagination and overflowing cup of personal paranoia. In fact, it was often cathartic. If she could imagine the very worst things that could happen to the planet, and devise potential responses to them, it robbed her own personal fears and troubles of their potency.

But not this time. Ed was gone. Three nights ago. The notification of divorce proceedings had been delivered to her this morning. *God*, that was fast. What was his hurry? Considering that Lennie hadn't suspected a thing until three nights and...twenty-three minutes ago. Maybe that was what hurt the most, that she'd been so blind. Lennie the genius, her friends called her. Not so smart, after all. Wrapped up in her work, imagining the most terrible things that could happen to a world, without realizing that sometimes 'the world' came down to just two people.

She ran her hands over her glossy black work-station. It was her link to the powerful computer nexus that produced the Reichmann Analog Virtual Environment — a long name with a catchy acronym was important to the people who wrote the cheques. Those grey-suited dark-tied backroom government autocrats had seen enough plain old supercomputers. They needed a name that could jazz up a bland requisition proposal and bamboozle a roomful of auditors. Lennie never used the full title. To her, the RAVE Nexus was part-taskmaster, part---playground. From its matrix of graphics imaging software, intelligent problem----solving, and pure brute processing speed sprang forth creations of startling realism. Lennie could step into a three-dimensional projection of a pristine globe, key in the disaster parameters, and watch it bleed in spreading pools around her.

As a biologist her specialty was pandemics. It was a sexy topic — had been since the first years of the century, for some reason. Scientists had latched onto the idea that pandemics followed some kind of regular schedule, and the world was overdue. After that it was a matter of course that every biological outbreak anywhere attracted an inordinate amount of attention from a global media fascinated with dying things. And if the scientific community found that modestly fanning the flames meant mounds of research money thrown their way, well, who could really blame them?

Lennie's job was to gather everything, from their most carefully assembled data to their wildest flights of fancy, and feed it to the RAVE-n. Then the cyber-mind was charged with assessing the probabilities of every scenario, analyzing the etiology, predicting the spread pattern, forecasting the fatality rates, yea, prophesying over the quick and the dead. They ran several scenarios a week. The human race had nearly been eradicated dozens of times.

Lennie and the RAVE-*n* were very good at their job.

Now, though, disaster had invaded her own reality. She felt it like a poison in her veins. Her vision lost its focus, and her fingers miscarried on the keys.

What had gone so wrong in the life they'd shared, she and Ed? (Eddy. She always called him Eddy because he called her Lennie. He was a sports writer, and everyone in that world was called Bobby or Jimmy or Scotty, weren't they? He dreamed of being a political reporter. Would he have called the President Barry?)

The screen was angrily flashing an image at her.

It was the corporate logo of the Reichmann Analog Corporation: a representation of the Pallas Athena, goddess of war and wisdom. *Damn.* She entered the 'SAFE' code to reset the security function. She had to concentrate, or the RAVE-n would kick her ass. And deservedly so. It wasn't just computer modeling that the RAVE-*n* controlled. All of Level Seven was a full-blown Hazmat lab, operated robotically. The substances studied in there were so dangerous that humans rarely ventured inside, except for the PhD equivalent of janitorial work. The test-tubes and beakers and petri dishes belonged to the RAVE-*n*. Inside were samples of Rickettsiae bacteria, the villain behind typhus and Rocky Mountain spotted fever; Arenaviridae viruses responsible for Lassa fever; Ebola virus; the corona virus that produced SARS; Marburg virus; several different strains of avian type A influenza viruses of the H5, H7, and H9 subtypes capable of infecting humans, and even a few precious grams of the 1918 Spanish Flu, culled from a corpse frozen in the Alaskan permafrost. Some of the most deadly pathogens known to humankind, all held in the capable pincers of a cybernetic brain and its robotic minions. It was the stuff of sci-fi fright movies, but Lennie wasn't worried. The RAVE-*n* had the abilities of an Artificial Intelligence in many ways, but no independent thought. She liked to say that even if the supercomputer *could* take over the world, the RAVE-*n* was too smart to *want* it.

No, there was far more danger from humans screwing up, maybe because they couldn't keep their inconvenient emotions from getting in the way. Lennie reached for a cup of coffee that was hours cold, and put it back down with a grimace.

They were running simulations of avian flu outbreaks again this week. Although it had been years since the first flare-ups of the H5N1 strain in Hong Kong in the late 1990's, and the more frightening outbreaks later in Southeast Asia, the best minds said that H5N1 or something like it was still lurking in the shadows, waiting for its moment to strike. Every so often it would appear in a flock of domestic fowl somewhere around the globe, and a massive slaughter would follow.

There hadn't been a documented case of H5N1 human-to-human transmission beyond one secondary victim. It was a pandemic held in check because the virus couldn't yet spread among the human population. But flu viruses mutate like there's no tomorrow.

A flock of wild ducks might fly over a poultry farm, leaving behind a bombardment of infected droppings. Wandering chickens would spread the virus to the nearby stock of pigs, one or two of which had already been unlucky enough to pick up a dose of *human* flu from the overly attentive Farmer Nguyen. Once inside the accommodating blood stream of the swine, the two visiting viruses could swap a few genes and, Presto: a new strain of bird flu capable of spreading among homo sapiens. Within a few days Farmer Nguyen and his family would have ruined lungs, filled with blood, as their bodies' misguided immune systems deployed cellular soldiers that destroyed the very tissues they were meant to save.

In the outside world the process of mutation was random and slow. It was a different story among the gleaming white walls of Level Seven. There a macabre array of stainless steel bones danced within Plexiglas cylinders, slicing and dicing and splicing, finding new recipes of DNA — shiny new double strands of nucleotides mixed and matched from human diseases and those of the animal kingdom, with the deliberate purpose of *creating* new pathogens deadly to humans. The rationale was that, by creating these lethal agents we could learn how to fight them.

Lennie was always grateful that she didn't tend to remember her dreams.

She also felt that her own hands were clean. She didn't create the murderous agents. She only ran simulations of their path of destruction.

When she and the RAVE-*n* turned the new killer loose, it was only on a *virtual* globe — an ethereal construct of numbers and electrical impulses, sanitized and safe. Lennie provided the data and the computer showed her Armageddon.

She would never admit it to anyone, but it was morbidly fascinating to watch the world's dominant species die a thousand gruesome deaths. Particularly if at least one of the virtual victims bore the face of Eddy.

No, that wasn't true. She didn't want him dead. Maybe the blame was hers. She'd always known that secrets could tear a relationship apart. Her father's military career had poisoned her parents' marriage after he'd been promoted into the upper echelons of the Pentagon, and had to hide the details of his workday from his own wife. After that, the trust was gone and the fire along with it — Lennie had watched it happen.

She'd vowed never to make the same mistake, but that was exactly what she'd done. It wasn't just her job's security demands; she'd told herself she was protecting Eddy from the horrors of Level Seven for his own good. It wasn't healthy to live day after day with the threat of a biological holocaust hanging like a Sword of Damocles in the mind's eye. Some people simply couldn't take it, and spent the rest of their lives in therapy.

So she couldn't tell him about her work, and she couldn't tell him why not. But he wasn't a fool. He suspected something. Eventually it turned into the conviction that she was involved in something big...a potential hot story that could be his *entrée* into the political arena. She was sure he hadn't come up with that idea on his own. It had the perfumed taint of that blonde internet blogger he'd talked about more and more often. The one who was always digging for government conspiracies. The one with the inflated ego and the inflated chest...

God! Was that what had happened? Had an online correspondence sparked an offline romance? *Oh Eddy... Eddy...did I drive you to that?* She felt a hot tear well up, and had to snap her head away before it could splash onto the keyboard.

She didn't want him dead. She was furious, cruelly hurt, and hopelessly infatuated all at the same time. She loved him beyond reason, and even now she knew that she would take him back without hesitation, if he asked. But what were the odds of that? Predicting them would take more skill than she had. It would require a master of predictions...

No. No, the idea was ridiculous. She turned her head away from the screens and imprisoned her hands beneath her legs to restrain them, while she rocked back and forth in confusion.

There was no-one else in the lab. There likely wouldn't be for another forty-five minutes — her coworkers liked to take long lunches. And she knew how to erase almost all traces of her commands, except in the RAVE-*n*'s deepest core memory.

Did she dare...?

Inevitable as a pandemic itself, she surrendered seven minutes later and furtively began to key in the data. The RAVE-*n* already had reams of information about Lennie. She quickly fed it a rough profile of Eddy, warts and all, resisting the powerful temptation to embellish the warts.

Query: *Will Lennie and Eddy get back together?*

There was no sign of activity from the RAVE-*n* — there never was. But sixty seconds was an eternity of processing time for a task that involved no global modeling, no quantum variables, and no fancy graphics in 128-bit studio-precision color.

The screen finally came to life.

RAVE-*n*: *Insufficient data.*

She exhaled a long-held breath and realized that her hands were trembling. She didn't dare try it again. It was sheer idiocy to have done it in the first place. She spent the next five minutes covering her tracks.

The rest of the afternoon was excruciating. Each time someone came over to speak to her, she expected them to hiss a withering accusation about using lab facilities for a personal whim. She vowed that she would never give in to such an unworthy impulse again. She hurried home that night in relief, and dreamed of a spinning globe projected in mid-air, with her face on one side and Eddy's on the other, and she could only watch helplessly as scenario after scenario brought spreading patches of emptiness like a cancer between them.

At the first coffee break the next morning, she asked again.

RAVE-*n*: *Insufficient data.*

This time she didn't delete the query, she merely hid it behind layers of other tasks. But it waited there for her to call it up, first at lunch, then at afternoon break, and eventually whenever she had the room to herself. In between, her mind would wander from cross-indexing fatality rates to trying to recall any memories of her marriage that might help in her cupidean quest.

RAVE-*n*: *Insufficient data.*

In frustration she nearly pounded a fist on the keyboard, but that might trigger another computation. Because of the dynamic interface, the machine already finished most of her sentences for her — they'd worked together for so long it anticipated nearly every keystroke. Instead she chastised herself again for obsessing over a husband (*EX* — husband!) and tried to force her tense fingers to relax on the keys.

She was startled to see the screen begin to fill with words...words beginning with EX...

Exacerbate

Exact

Exacting

Exaggerate

She quickly keyed in a 'Terminate' command. The RAVE-*n* was getting too damned helpful for their own good.

But not helpful where it really counted. Why couldn't the supercomputer produce an answer for *her*? Why didn't it even try?

The question was too simple — that must be it. She needed to approach it like any other scenario. Build a model, enter the data, run the simulation. But that would take time. She could never accomplish that much in a couple of coffee breaks. She had to...

She had to work overtime. Which meant she needed a cover story. Say her last pandemic simulation had run into bugs — of the computer, not biological variety — but she was close to tracking them down and didn't want to lose the momentum?

Her supervisor accepted the fiction readily enough. Lennie was one of his best workers. And anyway she was on a salary.

She had to be careful. There was still a possibility that someone else might be working late and walk in on her. It was even possible that one of the security people would make a random check on her work station. She needed a shadow screen — a secondary display she could bring up with a stroke of a key. Only a real task would be convincing enough to fool a colleague, but she'd just finished the last of her most recent series of simulations. What else would look plausible?

She called up the RAVE-*n*'s latest results from Level Seven. And instantly regretted it. A quick scan of the data caused the blood to drain from her face.

Good God. This was the worst one yet: a strain of virus that appeared to be based on a hemagglutinin 5 and neuraminidase 1, but had stitched-on RNA from half a dozen sources. The testing just completed that afternoon showed a startling 100% lethality — virtually unheard of. Early indications revealed a six or seven-day incubation period, followed by fatality within four days. That alone made it much more dangerous than killers like Ebola — they killed their hosts so quickly that they rarely spread very far from the original source of the infection. This new creation had no such weakness. It was the perfect traveler. *God help us if...*

She didn't let her mind complete the thought. Instead she began the practiced routine of building the computer model that would complete it for her. The horrific allure of the new pathogen was nearly enough to distract Lennie from her original purpose.

It was the moment when the world could have been saved. But destiny or fate or evolution dictated otherwise. The pull of her aching heart was stronger. Once the basic parameters of her scenario had been established, she allowed the RAVE-*n* to fill in the rest, adding only the simple command to Run the program and then Terminate. Then she turned back to her private project. The reunion of Lennie and Eddy. The *best* case scenario.

*   *   *

It happened only minutes before midnight. She awakened to the sound of the alarms, and the pain where the keys had become embedded in her cheek.

Had they caught her?

The klaxon reverberated through the room, piercing her ears until her jaw ached. Warning lamps painted the walls in spasms of color. Finally gathering her wits together she snapped her head up to look at what they called "The Big Screen", a liquid crystal panel mounted from the ceiling that displayed announcements for all staff, and alerts of any kind. It was mutely screaming in giant fluorescent letters.

There was a breach on Level Seven. A deadly toxin was loose. Already an army of biohazard experts would be scrambling into hazmat suits — she could picture them racing down echoing hallways to bring the enemy to battle. Yet, even as she watched, her initial alarm turned to helpless horror.

The vents were opening!

The outside vents of the lab were intended to exhaust toxic gases in the event of a fire. They were a dangerous necessity, but there were countless failsafe systems to prevent them ever opening in the aftermath of a spill — exactly the kind of accident she was now witnessing. The failsafes could not be overridden manually by a murderous saboteur or terrorist maniac. That had been demonstrated again and again, before the lab could even be built. No-one could open the vents to the open air once a breach alert had been sounded.

No human.

The RAVE-*n*! The computer must have allowed it. Good God, could it have been caused by something she'd done?

Her fingers flew frantically over the keyboard, recalling the recent list of commands and actions, luminous letters reflected in her wet eyes.

No! It wasn't possible!

The last command line accused her from the screen like an executioner's pointing finger:

"Run program. EX-Terminate."

She slumped back in the chair, and her vacant eyes came to focus on the holographic globe suspended in mid-air before her, running its final simulation.

Blotches of invading crimson ate their way hungrily around the ghostly blue projection of her home world, almost more quickly than she could see. In a daze, she tapped a trio of keys to check the time scale and drew a ragged breath, then expanded the range to slow the simulation down. This time she could see the wash of salmon color, representing the transmission of the virus, racing around the globe in a flash. Immediately afterward followed the blood red flood of fatality, moving slowly for the first ten or fifteen seconds, then almost instantly transforming the whole mottled Earth into a pulsing red beacon of warning. Stunned, she stood and walked into the center of the projection, then turned slowly in place, and swept her gaze over each quadrant. There was nowhere left untouched, no safe haven of shelter or resilience. Not even in the Himalayas, or the desert of the Sudan, or the barren Antarctic.

A flicker of movement drew her attention back to the Big Screen overhead. Its glaring fluorescent letters had been replaced with an epitaph of damning words.

Query: *Will Lennie and Eddy get back together?*

Quoth the RAVE-*n*: *Nevermore.*

ABOUT THE AUTHORS

Sean Costello is the author of nine novels and numerous screenplays. His novel **Here After** has been optioned to film by David Hackl, director of *Saw V*. Depending on the whims of his muse, Costello's novels alternate between two distinct genres: Horror and Thriller. His horror novels have drawn comparisons to the works of Stephen King, and his thrillers to those of Elmore Leonard.

You can learn more about Sean at www.seancostello.net

Mark Leslie is a writer, editor, and all around book nerd. His first published horror story "Phantom Mitch" received honorable mention in **The Year's Best Fantasy and Horror** and his first non-fiction book of true ghost stories, **Haunted Hamilton** was nominated for the Hamilton Literary Awards. Mark's fiction, which borders on horror, science fiction, and urban fantasy, has been described as "Twilight Zone" in style.

You can learn more about Mark at www.markleslie.ca

As the host of a radio morning show for most of his 30 years in broadcasting, **Scott Overton** has turned his skills to writing compelling near-future visions full of human potential and a sense of wonder. Scott's science fiction thriller, **The Primus Labyrinth** has been described as mind-bending and perfect for filling the void left behind for fans of Michael Crichton.

You can learn more about Scott at www.scottoverton.ca.